Praise for
The Second Life of Jack and Jackie

"*The Second Life of Jack and Jackie* is more than simply a book or a vision—it's a direct connection to the very essence of what makes us human. This love story between two icons masterfully bypasses all the standard cliches and tropes, traveling directly into your heart with honesty, raw emotion, and a feeling that you're right there, living this alternate life with them through the decades. Addressing one of the great "what ifs" of American history, this tale does so with grace, elegance and beauty. 10/10."

GEOFF WOLINER AUTHOR, *THE PATH TO PERFECTIA* SERIES

"I loved Melissa Kaplan's debut novel, *The Girl Who Tried to Change History*, so I was excited to read *The Second Life of Jack and Jackie*. In this novel, Melissa speculates about what would have happened had Jack Kennedy not been assassinated but instead lived well into old age, and been married to Jackie for forty years. The storyline and dialogue are so realistic that I had to remind myself that this was fiction. And the last few chapters, in which Melissa describes Jackie's terminal cancer and death, are powerful and touching. They literally gave me goosebumps!"

DIANE PAPALIA ZAPPA AUTHOR OF
THE MARRIED WIDOW: MY JOURNEY WITH BOB ZAPPA
AND *DEAR BOBBY: MY GRIEF JOURNEY*

I0637166

"I loved escaping into an alternative version of this famous couple's history. It is wonderful to imagine what Jack and Jackie's life could have been had he survived the 1963 assassination. Thank you, Melissa Kaplan, for penning a beautiful story of hope and resilience captured through the voices of the beloved Kennedys."

MARIA LEONARD OLSEN PODCASTER AND AUTHOR OF
50 AFTER 50: REFRAMING THE NEXT CHAPTER OF YOUR LIFE

The Second Life of
Jack and Jackie

The
Second
Life of
Jack
and
Jackie

a novel

Melissa Kaplan

BOLD
STORY
PRESS

CHEVY CHASE, MARYLAND

Bold Story Press, Chevy Chase, MD 20815
www.boldstorypress.com

First edition: April 2025
Library of Congress Control Number: 2025903090
ISBN: 978-1-954805-72-9 (paperback)
ISBN: 978-1-954805-73-6 (e-book)

Cover and interior design by KP Books

Printed in the United States of America
10　9　8　7　6　5　4　3　2　1

Of all the women I've ever known,
there was only one I could have married—
and I married her.
JOHN F. KENNEDY

I should have guessed that it would be
too much to ask to grow old with
and see our children grow up together.
JACQUELINE BOUVIER KENNEDY ONASSIS

None of this happens, of course.
Or it does happen, but not so you would notice.
It happens in another dimension of space.
MARGARET ATWOOD, *THE BLIND ASSASSIN*

Imagine, for a moment, that history took a different turn on November 22, 1963. What might have happened if President John F. Kennedy survived the bullet that struck him in Dallas, and, instead of their story ending so tragically that day, he and Jackie had the opportunity to continue their journey together over the next three decades?

This novel is an attempt to tell that story, or one possible version of it, and explore the possibilities of an alternate version of history. This fictional story of Jack and Jackie's marriage is bound not by fact but by the ideas of love, resilience, and how we choose to shape our own destinies.

Contents

Prologue

The New York Times
May 20, 1994

Jacqueline Bouvier Kennedy, Former First Lady, Dies at 64

Jacqueline Bouvier Kennedy, the former First Lady who presided over a renaissance of the arts and a famous restoration of the White House during her husband's presidency, died yesterday from complications from cancer. She was 64.

Mrs. Kennedy was among the youngest and most popular first ladies in American history. During her eight years in the role, she made the Kennedy White House a magnet for artists and creatives and completed an extensive restoration of the executive mansion to highlight its history. During her post-White House years, she began a career in publishing, working as a book editor first at Viking Press and then at Doubleday, where she continued working until her death.

Mrs. Kennedy died surrounded by her family, including her husband of forty years, former President John Fitzgerald Kennedy, and their three children. Also at her bedside during her final hours were her brothers-in-law, former President Robert F. Kennedy and Senator Edward Kennedy, as well as other family and friends.

Mrs. Kennedy will be buried at Arlington National Cemetery on Monday, May 23. (See article on p. 23 Style section for more about Mrs. Kennedy's life and legacy).

Part One

The Beginning

1963–1964

Chapter One

J ack, what do you think you're doing?"

Her voice stopped him as he attempted to rouse himself from the hospital bed, and he fell back against the pillow in resignation. "Nothing."

"You shouldn't be moving. Just lie still for once, will you please? What do you need?"

She walked quickly from the doorway of the hospital room and sat down on the edge of his bed. She was still wearing the same pink suit she'd had on yesterday, the one he'd asked her to wear for him as it had always been his favorite. She hadn't changed yet; she hadn't gotten a chance. Since the moment he'd been brought to the hospital, she hadn't left his side until now.

"Just some water. Thanks."

She reached over and poured some into the glass that had been just out of his reach. How easily they slipped back into these roles, he mused; him lying helpless in a hospital bed while she took care of him. His mind wandered back to the first year of their marriage, a decade ago now, when he had almost died in another hospital on an operating table, when their life together had barely begun.

And yesterday, once again, it had almost ended.

"I just spoke with the doctor," she said, reaching out to take the glass back from him after he had gulped down the water she'd offered. "He says you're going to be fine."

For the first time since they'd arrived at the hospital yesterday, she smiled at him, and he could see the relief in her eyes.

"Of course I am. The bullet barely grazed me." This was true for the most part, but he had to admit that being shot at was not a comfortable experience even if he realized things could certainly have turned out much worse.

She continued as if he hadn't spoken. "The doctor said there was some significant blood loss, which is why they had to give you the transfusions. But he thinks you'll recover just fine, assuming you take it easy and don't overtax yourself."

"Well I'll try, but you know I do have a country to run." He tried to sit up again but winced as the wound in his shoulder issued a stabbing pain, a reminder of yesterday's near-miss. As if he needed anything to remind him of what had happened just twenty-four hours ago.

They had been riding through the streets of Dallas on the second day of their whirlwind Texas tour, a rapid sprint through unfriendly territory. He was unpopular in Texas, and he knew it. But Texas was critical for his reelection hopes next year, so there they were, cruising through the streets lined with people, the blazing sun beating down on them, making him squint as he waved out at the crowds that thronged the road.

It was a better reception than he had been expecting. Everywhere they had been over the last two days the crowds had been large and enthusiastic, bringing back to him the exhilaration of the campaign trail from years ago. There was something special about being at the center of crowds like this, even in such an unlikely setting, and he had to admit it raised his spirits considerably after the gloom-filled few months he'd just endured.

Of course, he knew they weren't there solely to see him. As he waved from the car, top down and sunshine pouring from the sky, he could hear the crowds on the other side of the street breaking into an almost ecstatic cheer as they called out her name: "Jackie! Jackie!"

The rapturous crowds were no surprise to him; it was always like this when they traveled together. He had only been half-joking two years ago when he had introduced himself as "the man who accompanied Jacqueline Kennedy to Paris." That first big overseas trip as President had been a mixture of success and disastrous failure for him, but it had been purely a triumph for her. Wherever they traveled around the globe together, he was aware by now that he was only part of the package; people lined up to see her as much as him.

That was why she was in Dallas with him that day; at least it was part of the reason. Just a few weeks ago when she'd returned home from her trip to Greece, he'd cautiously broached the subject one morning over breakfast.

"I'd like you to come to Dallas with me to campaign," he had said, more tentatively than usual. He knew it wouldn't normally be an opportunity she would jump at. She generally dreaded campaigning; navigating the crowds that invigorated him was often an ordeal for her. But he knew having her there could make all the difference. Texas might not love him, but the whole country—the entire world—loved her.

She looked thoughtful and took a moment to reply, seeming to mull over his request. He wanted her to understand why he was asking, why this was so important to him. He continued, "Texas will be a tough sell next year, Jackie. And I think your being there with me will really help."

What he meant but didn't say: *I need you.*

She nodded, then said, "Of course, Jack. If you want me to go with you to Texas, I'll do it."

He smiled in surprised relief; he had anticipated a much more difficult conversation. He hadn't expected her to agree so easily. But maybe, after all they'd been through together during the past few months, he shouldn't have been so shocked. Something had shifted between them, and her ready acquiescence to his request seemed in keeping with their new, deeper connection.

"Thank you." He took her hand across the breakfast table and smiled, trying to express his appreciation in this small gesture. She smiled back, and he began to feel better. About Texas. About the future. About everything that lay ahead.

———

When the first shot rang out, it sounded like a firecracker.

Or at least, that was how he would always remember it, even decades later when his thoughts drifted back to the day he had almost died. Again.

The loud crack shattered the bright sunny afternoon, breaking through the cheerful noise of the crowd around them. It took him a moment to realize what the sound was, and even then he didn't quite believe it. Although he had known something like this could happen, somehow he hadn't really thought it would. Not even here in Texas.

But then the second shot slammed into him. Later he would claim it only grazed his shoulder, but in fact the bullet hit the artery in his neck, and within seconds he could feel its sting and the blood beginning to pour out of him as he fell over and slumped into her lap.

"Jack! Jack!" He heard her voice, and it was the most beautiful and terrible sound he'd ever heard in his life. A thousand thoughts raced through his mind in those split seconds, a thousand visions of the future—their future—exploding before his eyes.

"Jack!" she cried again, pulling him into her lap and trying to shield him from wherever the shots had come from. He tried to sit up, to make sure she was okay, but he couldn't. His head was spinning, the wounds in his neck and shoulder felt as though they were on fire, and he was too dizzy to speak. But he heard the panic in her voice, her normally unflappable calm falling to pieces as she cradled his head in her arms, bending her body over his.

She thinks I'm dying, he realized. *Am I?*

No. This is not happening. This is not how this will end.

"Jackie," he muttered, speaking as loudly and clearly as he could, but his voice was drowned out by the screams of the people around him. He could hear Governor Connally and his wife in the front of the car, the terrible sounds coming from a few feet away from him, but he couldn't focus on them. He spoke again more loudly and tried to turn his head so she could hear him.

"Jackie. Are you okay?"

She heard him that time. He heard her gasp, then bend down, trying to look into his eyes while still shielding him from the danger above. "Jack? Can you hear me?

"Yes," he whispered, unsure if his words reached her. But she could hear him now. She was bent down over him, wrapping him so tightly in her arms that all the panicked noise around them seemed to dissipate; he could only hear her voice.

"Jack, are you okay? Jack, I love you—Jack?"

He forced himself to keep his eyes open, ignoring the stabbing pain in his neck and shoulder and trying not to think about the blood pouring out of him. He looked up and, seeing her face, tried to focus on that.

"I'm okay," he muttered. "Are you alright?"

"Yes—yes, I'm okay. We're going to the hospital. You'll be fine, Jack; you're going to be fine."

He felt his eyes close again as he struggled to stay conscious, not to give into the waves that were threatening to pull him under. His hand found hers, and he squeezed it and felt her squeeze back.

"It's going to be okay, Jack."

"I know," he murmured. His vision was darkening, and he knew he'd be unconscious in another minute, but he had just enough time to utter the words he needed to say to her before the tide of darkness rose up to consume him.

"I won't leave you, Jackie."

And with those words the darkness pulled him under, and he knew nothing more.

He tried to sit up again, and she helped him into a seated position and began fluffing the pillows behind him. He wasn't sure whether she was doing these things to make him more comfortable or to avoid thinking about the enormity of what had just happened. Probably it was a bit of both.

The anesthesia he'd been given was wearing off, and his mind felt less sluggish. Now, suddenly, a million thoughts were crowding his brain. He didn't know where to begin; there were so many things he wanted to say, so much he needed to tell her. He decided to start with questions.

"How are the kids? Where are they?"

"They're fine. They're at home now with Maud, and my mother's there as well. I told them we'd be home in a few days."

"What else did you tell them?" He winced as the pain in his shoulder flared as he shifted his position in the bed slightly.

"I said that you'd had an accident, so we would have to stay in Texas for a few more days. Caroline was very worried about you, but I told her you'd be just fine and would be home soon, and that seemed to cheer her up. John is mostly worried we might not be back in time for his birthday. I told him we'd try our very best to make it, but if not, we'll just have his party a few days later."

"Of course. No matter what happens, we can't miss his third birthday." The thought that he had come so close to missing his son's birthday—all his children's future birthdays—still chilled him as he thought about it. If the bullet had hit him a few inches higher, in the back of his head instead of his neck . . .

He wouldn't think about that. Not now. There were too many other things he needed to focus on.

"Do they know who the shooter was?" It felt so strange to ask that question, as if it were perfectly normal to be inquiring about the identity of his would-be murderer.

She looked down and took his hand, then gazed back up at him. "They've arrested someone. His name is Lee something. Oswald? There's another name in there, but I don't remember." She shook her head wearily. "Just some silly little communist, from what they told me. Bobby will be able to tell you more when he gets here."

"Good." He wasn't quite sure what he meant by that, but he wanted to move off the subject.

"How are you?"

"I'm fine." She said it too quickly as if by rote and smiled, but it was unconvincing.

"Jackie."

"What? I'm fine. I'm just so relieved you're going to be okay."

He sighed and shook his head. "I know you're trying to be brave, Jackie. But it would be a little more convincing if I couldn't see my blood on your suit."

She winced, and he immediately regretted his words; he hadn't meant them to sound so harsh. "I'm sorry. What I mean is—you were right there next to me when it happened. I can't even imagine what that must have been like for you. Jackie, I'm so sorry."

"Jack, don't be ridiculous. None of this is your fault!"

He sighed. Of course she was right, strictly speaking—but still. There were so many things he could have done differently, and not just yesterday. He paused and looked at her, trying to collect his thoughts to say what he needed to say.

"I just—I shouldn't have pushed for this trip. It was a stupid idea. It's not like we didn't know Texas could be dangerous. There were wanted posters up with my face on them, for God's sake. And we shouldn't have been riding in the car with the top down; it was too risky. We both could have been killed."

And if anything had happened to you because of me, I would never forgive myself, he added in his head. Not that he would have been able to forgive himself if he'd also been killed.

"Jack," she said softly as she reached out her hand to brush the hair off his forehead. "Listen to me. You are not responsible for the actions of a madman who tried to murder you, do you understand?"

He saw the fierce expression come over her face, and he knew she was thinking about how near he'd come to dying. Her own close call with mortality didn't seem to faze her nearly as much as the possibility that he might not have survived yesterday. Not for the first time in the past few months he thought to himself, *I don't deserve you.*

He never had, really. And on some level, perhaps he'd always known it. But as long as a man was alive, it was never too late for him to change. Yesterday had been a wake-up call for him, the biggest of his life, and he wasn't going to waste this opportunity. He was going to be different from now on. *They* were going to be different.

He took a deep breath and launched into the words he'd known he needed to say to her ever since he'd faded into darkness in the back seat of the car in her arms yesterday.

"I know all that, but still, Jackie, I'm sorry. Not just for what happened yesterday; I'm sorry for everything you've been through these past ten years. I know it hasn't been easy for you."

"For either of us," she corrected him gently and squeezed his hand. He knew she was thinking about Patrick right now, and it was true; the death of their baby son just three months ago had been shattering for them both. Even though it had brought them closer and helped heal some of the wounds of the past, the memory and the loss still ached.

"Yes. But I'm talking about you. I nearly died yesterday" *(again,* he thought silently*)*, "and if I had, there are so many things I would have regretted not ever having the chance to put right with you."

She gazed at him with a startled expression on her face.

"What I mean is—the past few months have been hard for both of us. But for our whole marriage, I've made things much harder for you than I should have. I've made a lot of mistakes, Jackie, we both know that. I've put you through so much, and so many times I wasn't there when you needed me to be." *Arabella,* he thought, remembering how seven years ago he'd failed to show up for her in any sense after their first daughter was stillborn. The memory flooded him with shame, and he struggled to keep his voice steady.

"Jack," she said softly, twining her fingers with his and squeezing his hand. "I forgave you for all of that long ago."

"But you shouldn't have had to forgive me. Because it never should have happened. And then I kept making things worse." He shook his head, reflecting in that moment on all his past transgressions. All the other women in his life, his many dalliances over the course of their marriage. She had known, and pretended not to mostly, but of course he'd realized she knew what was happening. But that was what they did, what they had done for years: sidestepped, avoided, not talking about the uncomfortable truths that lay beneath the surface of their marriage, as perfect as it might look to the outside world. But he knew the truth, and so did she. He looked back now at that not much younger version of himself and felt nothing but disgust.

How could I have done that to her, over and over? How could I have let it go on for so long when I knew how it was hurting her?

And yet she'd stayed with him, despite everything. And now here she was, sitting beside him, holding his hand, more upset that she'd almost lost him to a gunshot yesterday than that she'd nearly lost her own life.

"I don't deserve you, Jackie." He spoke these words, the simplest of truths, because he didn't know what else to say to her.

She didn't say anything, just gazed steadily at him with unreadable eyes. Maybe she didn't know how to respond to his words, to hearing him say aloud all these things he'd never acknowledged to her before. But then, suddenly, she spoke.

"Well, maybe you're right." She smiled, and he actually saw a mischievous light in her eyes, an expression he hadn't caught there in years, since the long-ago days when they'd first begun dating. "'But I'm afraid you're stuck with me, either way."

"Thank God," he said, squeezing her hand back. She bent down and leaned against him, carefully avoiding his bandaged shoulder, and closed her eyes, sighing as she curled into his side, and he wrapped his uninjured arm around her.

It felt like everything was right with the world, with the two of them. But he knew it wasn't yet; there was one more thing he had to tell her, one more promise he needed to make.

"Jackie, I swear to you—from now on, things will be different. I'll never hurt you again. Never."

He couldn't force out any more words as his eyes began to fill up with unshed tears. But men like him were not supposed to cry, at least not after their own brushes with death. Tears were allowed only when facing the loss of someone he loved.

He hadn't told her everything he'd meant to, but when she moved her head and he saw her smile through her own tears, he knew it had been enough. Almost enough.

"I love you, Jackie," he whispered, closing his eyes as he felt the exhaustion of the past twenty-four hours seep into his bones.

She wrapped her arms around him, tucked her head underneath his chin. "I love you too. Always."

And with those words—exchanged in a bleak white hospital room in Dallas, Texas, after a long turbulent decade filled with highs and lows, sorrows and joys, love and pain—their marriage began anew, a day after it had almost ended. A few inches in a bullet's trajectory, a few words spoken at long last, and the future was transformed completely.

Life is funny that way.

Chapter Two

The White House
December 25, 1963

I t was nearly midnight; in a few moments, Christmas would be over. The house looked like a holiday explosion, tinsel and lights decorating the rooms, poinsettias covering the tables, the floor still strewn with boxes and wrapping paper from this morning's present opening. They had opted to stay at the White House for Christmas rather than travel to Palm Beach; his doctors had advised he would do better to stick closer to home this year, just in case. He hadn't argued with them. One month away from an attempted assassination, he didn't see any harm in being cautious for once.

After all the turbulence of the past few months, this Christmas had felt like a gift. Not simply because he was there to see it, as he so nearly hadn't been, but because it offered him a bit of a break from showing up to work every day and trying to convince people he was okay. He knew everyone around him meant well, but their sideways glances at him, the constant sense that he was being watched and monitored as he recovered from his gunshot wounds and returned to normal life, became more than a little wearying after the first few days.

It had been nearly a month now since he'd gotten out of the hospital, ultimately no worse for wear after the shooting, though his back was still killing him. But he supposed he couldn't really blame his would-be assassin for that.

It was this kind of dark humor that he'd drawn on in the weeks after the shooting to show the country, the world, that he wasn't afraid. After all, there was still a Cold War on, and Americans liked their leaders to be strong and fearless, to laugh in the face of danger.

So he'd done his best, concealing from everyone how shaken the incident had left him feeling inside. And for the most part, people seemed to believe him, perhaps simply because they wanted to. The country had responded to his attempted assassination with a massive outpouring of support: the White House had received half a million cards and a staggering number of flowers, most of which had been donated to local hospitals and churches because the building simply couldn't hold them all. And his approval rating had rocketed overnight to eighty percent. He was grateful for the support, but at the moment, at least for a few days during the holiday season, he wanted more than anything to push the memories of his recent near-death experience from his mind and just concentrate on something, anything, else instead.

He'd spent most of today with his children, which had been a wonderful relief. Caroline and John still didn't fully understand what had happened a month ago; he and Jackie had agreed they'd have to tell them at some point but had decided to wait until a bit more time had passed and life had returned to normal. Meanwhile, his children had enthusiastically welcomed him home upon his return from the hospital, and once they'd seen that he looked more or less the same as before, their worries about "Daddy's accident" had faded and they'd turned to the much more important business of preparing for Christmas—making their lists for Santa, decorating the tree, hoping for a Christmas Eve snowfall.

For him and for the children it had been a magical Christmas. Yet despite the copious holiday cheer that pervaded the house, something still felt off. He and Jackie had barely spoken all day—not because they were arguing but because they'd hardly had a moment alone to hold a conversation. Of course, they'd been together while the children opened their gifts, and at church, and sat beside one another at dinner, but all those times there had been other people around and no real chance to talk privately.

He had thought this was simply happenstance, but now, as the day wound down and Christmas neared its close, he wasn't so sure. She'd seemed particularly quiet today, withdrawn. Even as she smiled and exclaimed over Caroline's and John's gifts from Santa, she'd looked as though she was not truly celebrating but simply going through the motions. He'd tried to shrug off this feeling as he plunged into wholehearted enjoyment of the holiday with his children, but now that Caroline and John were tucked into bed and the house was quiet, Jackie was still nowhere to be found. He began to wonder if she was avoiding him—and if so, why?

He walked into her bedroom—or what used to be her bedroom—and found her at last. She was sitting at her vanity, brushing her hair with meditative precision. For their first three years in the White House, she had inhabited this room while he had slept next door. However, that had changed after their return from Dallas. The day they arrived back home after his release from the hospital, she brought him not to his own bedroom but to hers and announced with determined nonchalance, "I think you should stay here tonight. In case you need anything." And so he had. And he'd slept in this room with her every night since. Neither of them had mentioned it since that first day, but it was already clear to him that this was how things would be from now on. It was yet another effect of the events of last month on their marriage, but it was not one he had any complaints about.

And yet now, as he gazed at her while she performed this simple bedtime ritual, he realized that for the first time since the shooting she seemed distant, unreachable, and he didn't know why.

"Hi," he said, rather tentatively. She turned toward him, looking momentarily hesitant, then smiled. Yet there was still something wrong, something strange in her manner that he couldn't fathom.

"Sorry, I didn't mean to startle you."

"No, no. It's fine."

He sat down on the edge of the bed. "It was a great Christmas, wasn't it?"

"Oh yes. It was wonderful." The words were correct, but they sounded artificial, as though she were acting in a movie rather than having a real conversation.

"Is everything okay? I feel like I've barely seen you today."

"What do you mean? We've been together all day."

"With the kids and the family, sure. But not by ourselves."

"I'm fine. Really. It was a wonderful Christmas. About as perfect as it could be."

He sat on the bed, staring at the back of her head and glimpsing her face in the mirror—a mask, revealing no emotions. He knew something was wrong, but he had no idea what it was or how to break through the wall she seemed to have erected around herself.

She put down the hairbrush softly on the vanity, but she didn't rise from her chair. Then suddenly, she broke her silence. "Jack?"

"What is it, Jackie?"

"I can't stop thinking about him."

It took a split second for the realization to catch up with him, and then he understood.

Patrick.

Of course.

He felt instantly stupid for not having figured out the cause of her melancholy sooner. And hard upon that, he felt guilty—for being so happy today, for not thinking about their lost child, for willing the painful memories to stay away so that he could enjoy the holiday with his family and take a break from the crushing grief of the past few months.

But for Jackie, clearly, there had been no break. As she turned to look at him, tears welling up in her eyes, he saw the grief still heavy there, despite the holidays, the festivities of the day—even the miracle of his own survival.

He wanted to find the right thing to say to her, to make her feel better, but after a moment he realized there were no words that could possibly do that. Instead, he nodded. "I know. Neither can I."

She looked down, speaking in a low voice, choked with emotion. "All day long—I kept imagining him here with us. He'd be almost five months old now. Maybe he'd be sitting up, starting to crawl, playing with his Christmas gifts." She broke off for a moment before resuming. "This should have been his first Christmas. Our first Christmas together—the five of us—as a family. And instead—"

She shook her head, the rest of her sentence too painful to complete.

He rose and walked over to her. She stood up, and he pulled her into his arms. She rested her head against his chest, her voice muffled but the pain coming through clearly. "I'm sorry. Saying this to you—I feel so guilty."

He was startled and pulled back to look at her. "Why? Why would you feel guilty?"

She glanced up at him, her face tear-stained. "Because you're alive, Jack. You're still here. And I know how lucky I am, how close I came to losing you this year too. It's a miracle, and I should be grateful for it, and I am. You have no idea how much I am, but still . . ."

"I know," he murmured, stroking the back of her head. "One thing doesn't make up for the other."

"No." She sighed, burying her face against him.

After a moment, he said quietly, "If I could have taken his place, I would have."

"No," she said, shaking her head and looking up at him with the fierce expression he recognized from the morning after the shooting when they'd talked in the hospital. "Don't say that! Don't ever say that, Jack. If it hadn't been for you, I never would have made it through last summer. And if I'd lost you that day . . ." She took a deep breath, collecting herself. "I honestly don't know how I would have gone on. I don't think it's even possible that I could have, on my own."

He eased her gently onto the bed, and they sat there for a moment, arms wrapped around each other.

"I don't know how I'm ever going to get past it, Jack. I'm so sad, and so angry, and so . . . heartbroken. Yes, I know he's in heaven. He's fine. He's happy. But that doesn't make me feel any better. I'm his mother. I want him here with us, where he belongs. And when people tell me that he's with God—I know they mean well, but honestly, it makes me want to scream. Why should he be with God instead of here with us? He already took two of our children; why take Patrick as well? What did we ever do to deserve any of that?"

She broke down, sobbing in his arms, and he held her as tightly as he could as her body shook and the tears spilled out. His eyes began to well up, and he knew he wouldn't be able to hold his own tears back much longer.

He wanted to be strong for her, but after the past few months, he wasn't sure he had that kind of strength in him anymore—the kind he had used in the past to keep his feelings inside.

But maybe that was okay. Because they were here, together, sharing their grief and heartbreak, and he knew she was the one person who would understand.

Suddenly and unbidden, a question broke from him.

"Jackie? Can I ask you something?"

She looked up, wiping the tears from her face. "Yes?"

He paused for a moment, then said, "Tell me about Arabella."

Her face became very still except for the widening of her eyes. The tears were gone from them now, and she regarded him steadily. "What do you want to know?"

He thought for a moment, then replied, "Everything. Every single thing you can tell me about her."

She gazed at him for a moment with a look that was unreadable, and at first he wasn't sure she was going to answer. But then she began to speak. Her voice, which had cracked with emotion just moments ago, now sounded much calmer, as if she'd just been waiting for the moment when she could speak these words to him at last after so many years.

"Oh, Jack, she was so beautiful. Just absolutely perfect— like a little angel." And she spoke, her voice quiet but filled with love, about their stillborn daughter, the first child they'd never gotten to see grow up. The one he'd never even gotten to lay eyes on or hold, because he hadn't been there. Because he'd chosen not to be.

He'd been thousands of miles away, debauching and enjoying what he'd imagined would be his last few days of freedom before returning home to the responsibilities of family and fatherhood. The summer of 1956 had been a disappointing one for him as he campaigned for the vice-presidential nomination that, in the end, had proven just out of his reach. He'd felt angry, cheated, to see all his hard work come to nothing. If he had been wiser then, he would have realized that life was long, he was not yet even forty, and he had years ahead to make his White House dreams come true. And certainly he should have realized that he was about to experience a much greater joy than becoming a vice-presidential candidate: he was just weeks away from becoming a father. Or so he had believed.

He should never have left her; he knew that now. He should have stayed by her side with the birth of their first child approaching so soon. But he'd convinced himself that one last trip, one last hurrah, was in order before his life changed forever. She had told him she would be okay while he was gone and she would see him when he got back. And so he had left for Europe.

And then everything had fallen apart. The baby had arrived too early, and the doctors hadn't been able to save her. After getting the horrifying news about what had happened back home, he knew he should have rushed to Jackie's side to comfort her: it was the very least she'd deserved. Instead, he put off his return for days, unable to face the nightmare that he knew awaited him. He had finally returned, far too late, only after Bobby had called him and told him in no uncertain terms that he needed to come home and fix the mess he'd made.

When he arrived home, he expected her to be angry at him. She had every right. And when he walked through the door of their house that first day, he'd braced himself for her wrath, her fury. But instead he encountered something even worse—an icy silence. Her voice, usually so soothing and melodic, spoke in tones that were raspy and cold as she told him the bare details of what had happened in his absence and made clear he could make himself comfortable in the guest room, or out of the house if he preferred—as far away from her as he could possibly be.

After his return, she had frozen him out for months. Every time he tried to get her to talk about what had happened—to make some kind of inadequate apology—she simply refused to engage him. It had been months before they'd even reestablished themselves on normal speaking terms.

He'd borne with her silence, her frostiness, because he knew he deserved it. Indeed, he deserved far worse. But at the same time, he kept trying to forget. Forget the baby, the child he hadn't been there to see, who would never smile or crawl or walk into his arms. Forget the tragedy that she'd taken as her own cross to bear, silently implying that because he hadn't been present to experience it himself he had no business sharing in her grief. And he couldn't argue. She was right.

Eventually, however, she did soften towards him. They began speaking to one another again, and gradually, they found their way back to something approaching a normal footing. A few months later, she became pregnant with

Caroline, and despite their dreams having been dashed twice already, they began to hope that the third time would finally bring them a baby. In the fall of 1957, their precious daughter had been born, and they'd become a family of three and a few years later of four. Life had gotten immeasurably better from the day of Caroline's arrival, and their shared love for their children had held them together even during the darkest times in their marriage.

But they had never talked about Arabella again. They had never revisited that devastating loss, the one that had so nearly broken them forever. They moved forward, trying never to look back, to focus only on the future. Or rather, he had. He could see now that for Jackie, that long-ago loss had never completely healed. And for the first time, he realized the same was true for him.

As he finally asked the question he'd avoided for years, she spoke so lovingly of their lost little girl, describing her face and her hands and her soft downy hair and making him see the pictures in his mind's eye, even though he hadn't been there. And he realized that for so long he'd felt he hadn't deserved to share this grief with her.

But now, as they finally spoke the name of the other child who, like Patrick, they had never gotten to see grow up, he felt as though that old grief was emptying out of him. Before he knew it, he had begun sobbing, burying his face in his hands, and she wrapped her arms around his shoulders, murmuring, "Jack, Jack, it's okay."

"No." He managed to choke out the single word. "No, it isn't. It never was. Because I wasn't there with you and with her. And I should have been."

He turned his face to look at her, and, to his amazement, there wasn't a trace of anger or of the coldness he remembered from all those years ago. The expression in her eyes was one of love and, amazingly, understanding.

"You're right, Jack. I remember; I was there. And I'm telling you—it's okay now. You don't have to punish yourself anymore for what happened years ago."

He gazed into her eyes, grasping her words like a lifeline. "I don't understand."

"What don't you understand?"

He shook his head. "How you can say that. How you ever managed to forgive me after what I did."

She ran a hand over his hair and spoke in the gentlest of tones. "That's simple, Jack. Because I love you. And sometimes that's what love needs to be about—forgiveness."

"Even for things that are unforgivable?"

She shook her head. "I don't think any mistakes are unforgivable. Not after these past few years, and all we've been through. Once I might have thought that, but now . . ." Her voice trailed off. "Yes, I was angry at you after we lost Arabella. I won't lie to you about that. But time heals, at least some things. And as soon as Caroline was born and you held her in your arms for the first time . . ." She smiled, her eyes brightening at the memory. "I knew at that moment that you'd be a wonderful father, the best our children could possibly hope to have. And I was absolutely right."

He stared at her for a few moments in silence, taking in her words. He flashed back to the thought that had echoed in his brain the day after the shooting, when he'd awoken to see her at his side, smiling joyfully at the news that he would be all right, *I don't deserve you.*

Those words had proven true in their marriage many times. But the past didn't have to dictate the future, and he wouldn't let it. Looking into Jackie's face, as she managed to smile at him despite everything they'd been through over the years, he felt a surge of fresh determination to make a new start. He'd prove that he could be not just a good father but a good husband, no longer falling short and leaving her to pay the price. Those days were over now.

He was still too possessed by his roiling emotions to put any of this into words, but he wrapped his arm around her shoulder and pressed her against him; she squeezed his hand, and he could tell that she understood.

After a moment, she blinked away the last tears from her eyes, and, remembering his vow to be a better husband, he had the presence of mind to offer her his handkerchief. She dabbed at her eyes, still red-rimmed but clearer now, then turned to him with a shaky smile.

"Well, I guess this wasn't exactly the Christmas we planned, was it?"

He shook his head. "No. But maybe it was the one we needed."

She nodded, squeezing his hand again. "On the bright side, there's only one more week, and 1963 will finally be over."

"Yes. And next year will be better. I promise."

Of course, it wasn't a promise he could keep, and she knew that. But the unspoken sentiment beneath his words was clear to her—that whatever good or bad the new year would bring, they'd get through it together.

"Well, Jack, Merry Christmas and Happy New Year."

"Yes. And here's to a much better 1964."

"Believe me, I'm already counting the days."

He smiled at her and pulled her into his arms to celebrate the final hours of Christmas together.

Chapter Three

The room buzzed with excitement. It was only six-thirty in the evening, far too early for there to be any news, but the waiting had already begun. On television, Walter Cronkite was talking about polls, turnout, and various states that would be critical for victory tonight. The election-night anticipation and anxiety she remembered from all of her husband's past campaigns were in full swing for her, and whatever he claimed, she could see that he was also a nervous wreck on the inside.

As he stood up nervously to stretch his legs again, she pulled on his arm to get him to sit back down. "Stop pacing, Jack."

He turned to her and sat back down, half-smiling but clearly unable to completely relax.

"I'm fine. Really."

"Well, you should be. Because you are going to win in a landslide tonight." She smiled her most radiant smile, conveying her utter certainty about her prediction.

"Well, we don't know that, Jackie."

"Come on, Jack. The latest polls had you up by fifteen points. You are going to win, and then life can get back to normal. In fact . . ." she attempted to shift her position on the couch, moving her hand to her enormous stomach, "the only real question to be decided tonight is whether I'll make it through the evening without having a baby, or if we can hold that off for a few more weeks."

"Let's do one thing at a time, shall we?" He smiled back at her, and she could see some of the tension in his expression begin to ease.

She reached out and took his hand in hers, noting how exhausted he looked up close after the last final days of nonstop cross-country campaigning. At least after tonight, all of that would be behind them forever.

"It will all be fine, Jack." She leaned against him and put her head on his shoulder, unmindful of all the other people in the room, Kennedys and Bouviers and his Irish mafia pals, all eagerly or nervously anticipating the results that would come in just a few more hours. He squeezed her hand, and she felt in his grasp many unspoken words as they finally reached the end of this long, hard, exhausting, and yet wonderful year, the year they almost hadn't had the chance to spend together.

It had been a cold, blustery day in March when she'd given him the news about the baby. "Our Valentine's Day surprise," she had said, smiling at him as she relayed the news immediately after coming from the doctor.

He sprang to his feet; she knew his back was still hurting him as usual, but there was no trace of it now. He looked younger, transformed and almost carefree as he beamed at her.

"Jackie, that's wonderful." Her husband wasn't given to emotional displays—at least he hadn't been before everything that had transpired over the past few months—but now he pulled her into his arms, and she rested against him, her mind jumbled with excitement and worry, hope and fear. After a moment she pulled away to look at him, seeing the happiness in his eyes.

She had known he would be thrilled by the news. Whatever problems they had faced as a couple over the past decade, his love for their children was the one thing she never doubted. She was glad she could bring him this kind of joy, but as much as she wanted to, she couldn't fully share it herself. At least not yet.

His expression changed as he scanned her face, and she realized he must be reading some of her hesitancy in her eyes. She hadn't meant for him to see that. She'd wanted this to be a purely joyful moment, the one they deserved after all they'd been through over the past year. But it was those trials that had brought them closer, close enough that hiding her fears from her husband, as she might once have tried to do, wasn't an option anymore.

He knows. He knows me too well.

"What's wrong, Jackie?"

Ah, there it is.

She started to say "nothing," as she would have in the old days. Stay strong, calm, collected; keep the darker emotions inside where they were safe. But somehow she didn't have the strength or perhaps the desire to do that anymore. Instead, she simply spoke the truth.

"I'm scared."

His eyes searched her face as if he were trying to read her thoughts or put together a puzzle with the clues she was giving him to work with. "Scared of what?"

She was fairly sure that he knew the answer to his question. But in asking her anyway, he was giving her the chance to talk about it. And suddenly she realized just how badly she needed that.

She sighed. "Afraid that something will go wrong." *Again.*

He sat down again in his rocking chair. She knew that even these past few minutes of standing might have caused him pain if he was having one of his bad days. She seated herself in a leather chair next to his, almost close enough to touch, but not quite.

"This is the sixth time I've been pregnant, Jack. And we have two children."

The simple math that had shaped the story of her life. Their lives.

"Yes." He sighed, looking down at the floor, knowing there was nothing he could say to make that painful, unalterable fact hurt less.

She chose her next words carefully, trying not to dampen the joy that this moment should bring—*would* bring any couple who hadn't been through the things they'd been through.

"I know I—I shouldn't be so afraid. I know everything will probably be just fine, but if it's not . . " She paused, and her voice trembled as she spoke the next words, "Jack, I don't know how I'd make it through that again."

He didn't speak for a moment. Eventually she looked up to see him regarding her steadily, and she wondered if she would catch her own worries reflected back in his eyes, if she had ruined this announcement for him by giving voice to her deepest fears. *Should I have said nothing? Just let him have this moment, without anything to darken it before we've even absorbed that it's happening?*

It was so hard to know. Ever since Patrick's death and especially since Dallas, things had been better between them. Their bond felt stronger, their connection more solid, and she could feel her confidence in their marriage growing day by day. But if the cost of admission to their newfound closeness was honesty—not just in the sense of not lying, but telling each other the whole truth and not dancing around it—it felt like a language she was still learning. Ten years into their marriage, she was still trying to figure out how to share the deepest parts of herself with her husband, and he was attempting to do the same.

He spoke at last. "Jackie, I understand. And honestly . . ." He took a deep breath, then looked at her: "I'm scared too."

"You are?" She looked at him in astonishment.

"I mean, how could we not be? After . . . after what we've been through."

Baby Patrick's name hung in the air, and neither of them could speak it at that moment. But it rested between them not as a wedge but as a bridge, a connection.

"I'm sorry. I wish I didn't feel this way. I wish I could just be happy. I know everything will probably be fine, but . . ." She sighed, looking down and then back up at him. "I'm not sure how to do this, Jack. How to live every day for the next nine months knowing that something could go wrong and we could go through all that pain again."

Because if I lose another child, it might actually kill me.

She couldn't say that part out loud; she was too afraid to speak those thoughts into existence. Even their newfound honesty had its limits.

He reached out and took her hand, and she had the impression that, like her a moment before, he was choosing his words with care.

"I know I said I was scared, Jackie, and it's true. But still . . ." He paused for a handful of seconds, then said, "I think it's going to be all right this time."

"Really?" She gazed at him, unblinking, wanting so badly to believe what he was saying. Thinking that she would give anything for it to be true.

"Really. Because I think, after this last year, maybe the tide is starting to turn for us. Maybe we've made it through the hardest part of our lives, and now the good part is ready to begin."

She was silent as she thought about this. And she realized that for so long she'd been bracing herself for the next terrible thing that was going to happen to her, to them, to their family. Every tragedy had darkened her vision of what the future could hold. Even their narrow escape in Dallas, the horrific fate they had avoided by a miracle of split-second timing, didn't fill her with the happiness or relief that it should have. Instead, it only made her feel more afraid. *What's coming next for us? What's around the next corner? What new tragedy is just waiting to unfold?*

I can't live my life this way.

The realization hit her hard with a powerful rush of truth and clarity. She couldn't spend the rest of her life being afraid of the next horrible thing that might happen. She couldn't control the future; if she could, she would have altered so very many things about her past. But if she spent her life trapped in fear, she would never be able to enjoy the things she did have: the happy moments, the simple daily joys.

I want to be happy. We deserve to be happy.

Her husband had been quiet for several minutes as she reflected silently on all this, but now he spoke a few words that she would remember for the rest of her days on earth.

"I really think everything will be okay, Jackie. Because after all, life has a way of evening out."

She looked at him, smiling through the tears that were beginning to pool in her eyes. But for the first time in longer than she could remember, they weren't brought on by sadness or pain.

"You're right, Jack."

She stood up, closing the distance between them and wrapped her arms around him, resting her head against his shoulder as she had in the hospital room in Dallas a few months ago. In that moment she made a choice to let go. To stop being afraid. To believe in the happiness that the future could hold for the two of them.

———————

On July 4th they finally shared their joyful news with the world. She hadn't planned it, and neither had he. For the past several months the baby had been their secret. Of course, a few people had to know: members of their family, her doctor, her Secret Service agent Clint Hill. But they kept up public silence throughout the spring and into early summer.

"I know we can't keep it a secret forever," she told Jack as they celebrated his forty-seventh birthday on May 29. It would have been a perfect time to announce the news, and she had considered doing so, but in the end she couldn't bring herself to share their secret yet, to invite the eyes of the world and the media into the tiny universe of their growing family. "But I still don't feel ready to share it. I need a little bit longer."

And he smiled at her, nodding in understanding. "Take as long as you want. There's no rush. We'll tell everyone when we're ready."

As lovely as her husband's support of her desire for privacy was, he was wrong about one thing: at some point, there would be a need to rush, to get out ahead of the story before it broke of its own accord. Because unless she hid inside the White House until November, she couldn't conceal her pregnancy forever.

And on the Fourth of July, the day finally came when she realized that camouflaging her growing stomach was no longer a feasible option. She spent nearly ten minutes that afternoon struggling to zip herself into the dress she'd planned to wear for the Independence Day celebration they were holding on the White House lawn. Friends and family would be gathering in a few hours to watch the fireworks and to celebrate 188 years of America and just over seven months since the miraculous survival of its thirty-fifth president. It would be a party no one in attendance would ever forget.

But no matter how hard she twisted and contorted herself, the dress she'd planned to wear for the party wouldn't fit. She could have tried to find another one—something shapeless but stylish enough to attempt to keep her secret hidden a little longer—but looking down at her rapidly growing waistline, she knew it wouldn't work. There was no hiding this news from the world anymore.

And suddenly she didn't care. She didn't *want* to hide it. For these past few months she'd been so afraid of tempting fate, but day by day she was becoming more confident that her husband might be right—that this time, fate was on their side.

And so on July 4, 1964, Jack and Jackie emerged on the front lawn of the White House holding hands, and the First Lady stunned the crowd in a flowing, knee-length dark blue and red dress—an outfit that acknowledged the symbolism of America's birthday while also revealing that in a few months' time the country would welcome a brand-new citizen.

New Baby for the Kennedys!

Surprise! JFK and Jackie Reveal Her Pregnancy to the World at Fourth of July White House Bash

The Secret Is Out! Glowing Jackie Kennedy Shares Baby News with the Country on America's Birthday

As soon as the news broke, the furor began. Overnight, they were inundated with congratulations (which she accepted graciously), questions (which she politely declined to answer), and well wishes (which they both truly appreciated).

"Well, Jackie, you managed to upstage America on her birthday," her husband laughed the next morning at breakfast, tossing aside *The New York Times* with its eloquent headline blaring their news to the world. "Pretty impressive, really."

"Is it possible to upstage an entire country?" She smiled, resting her hand on her stomach, mercifully freed from its constraints in a proper maternity dress for the first time. "I'm not sure anyone can do that."

"Well, if anyone can, it's you," he replied, smiling at her. "But maybe we'll just say you upstaged the Founding Fathers instead. Because no one will remember yesterday as the anniversary of the signing of the Declaration of Independence when they have this news to talk about instead."

She laughed, and it felt so good to laugh. So good to have their secret out at last.

Day by day, as the beautiful hot summer faded into memory and the season rounded inevitably into fall, her pregnancy became less newsworthy as the presidential campaign picked up momentum. She was sorry that once again she would not be able to campaign actively for her husband to win a second term; just as in 1960 when she was expecting John, she knew she would mostly have to sit on the sidelines to conserve her energy and protect her baby from the stresses and exhaustion of the campaign trail.

But she did what she could. She recorded campaign commercials in both English and Spanish, urging wavering voters (of whom there seemed to be very few this time around) to support Jack's re-election. She consented to do a joint TV interview with her husband in the White House, where they talked about her restoration of the building and all that the First Couple hoped the next four years would bring for the nation. And when *Vogue* contacted her staff in September to ask her to do a photo shoot with her children—all three of them—after the baby arrived, on a whim she said yes. Day by day, her confidence in the future was rising, and she felt more strongly that this time it really was all going to be okay.

And before she knew where the year had gone it was November again, and she was sitting by her husband's side on a sofa, eight-and-a-half months pregnant, watching the television and awaiting the first signs of what the night's outcome would hold—for America, for her family, and for the future.

The first returns began trickling in around 8 pm. Massachusetts, New York, Virginia, North Carolina, Florida, Ohio, Illinois, all fell into line like a row of dominos, carried easily by the incumbent. Long before the West Coast results were in, it was clear that all of Jack's worries had been for naught. This was more than a solid reelection victory; it was an historic landslide of epic proportions.

Even Texas eventually came through, after all the angst the Lone Star state had caused them just a year ago. "I'll give you full credit for Texas, Jackie," her husband said, squeezing her hand as he sat hunched over beside her, watching the television screen intently as the news reports rolled in. "I couldn't have done it without you."

"Well, it's the very least they owed you down there," she murmured. "But I'm glad I could help." She smiled as she felt the baby kick energetically as if he or she was bursting to celebrate this night with the rest of the family.

By 11 pm, the call was official: John F. Kennedy had been reelected as President of the United States.

When Walter Cronkite made the announcement, the room burst into applause and cheers, champagne bottles were popped open, and the joyful crowd was ready to celebrate what felt like both a political victory and an affirmation of all they'd worked so hard for over the past four years. After coming so close to having their dreams shattered in the most heartbreaking way last November, this moment felt more richly satisfying than they could have imagined even a few short months ago.

Soon, after a whirlwind of excited congratulations, it was time to leave the privacy of the viewing room and greet the crowds in the ballroom next door. A raucous victory party was already shaping up, waiting for the newly reelected president to join in the celebration.

Ordinarily, she loathed crowds, and would have been perfectly content to remain comfortably ensconced in the family bubble for the rest of the evening. But as Jack rose and held out his hand to her, with a smile on his face that was unlike any she'd ever seen from him before, she knew perfectly well that she wouldn't have missed what was coming next for anything in the world.

"Ready, Jackie?" he asked. She nodded, and he carefully helped her to her feet (no easy task these days, as her balance was getting trickier by the moment). Hand in hand, they walked over to the center of the room where Caroline and John, allowed for this special occasion to stay up long past their bedtimes, were feasting on candy from bowls strewn across the long buffet table. She'd given up trying to keep track of how much sugar they'd consumed this evening; she could go back to being a fastidious mother tomorrow morning. Tonight was special. Tonight was a celebration.

"Caroline, John, are you ready to celebrate Daddy's victory?" She smiled at both her children, and they laughed happily, running up to hug their father. He bent down as best he could and wrapped his arms around them both, then took Caroline's hand. She grasped John's, and the four of them walked together into the adjoining room.

"Ladies and gentlemen," a deep, booming voice announced as they crossed the threshold into the ballroom,

"May I present the President and First Lady of the United States!"

As they entered the room, the noise of the crowd exploded like nothing she'd ever heard. She had thought she was immune to the sound of crowds by this point, that she'd seen it all and heard it all over the past four years, but she was wrong. This was a roar of victory, of celebration, of pure, unfiltered joy unlike anything they'd experienced before. She couldn't help smiling, and she couldn't remember the last time she'd smiled so widely and authentically, especially with so many people present and so many photographers setting off flashbulbs that burst on and on around her and her family. Normally, this was the thing she enjoyed least about being the wife of the president.

But tonight everything felt different. This was a celebration for them, for their family, for the entire country. A celebration of survival, resilience, and the triumph of good over evil, hope over fear, life over death.

This was the celebration her husband deserved, and she felt her heart almost bursting with pride and happiness for him.

Well done, Jack.

She beamed at him as he stepped up to the podium, acknowledging the roar of the crowd and the waving signs, American flags, and chants echoing through the building, *"JFK! JFK! JFK!"*

It took nearly five full minutes for the crowd to subside into silence, though of course she didn't count the minutes at the time. It was a minor historical detail that future biographers would someday record when they wrote about this victory night. All she knew was that for once she felt she could have stood listening to the raucous, joyful crowd forever and never wanted the celebration to end.

Finally the audience's cheers subsided, and her husband began to speak. The words, painstakingly crafted by his speechwriter Ted Sorenson, rolled out as elegantly as she would have expected. The speech was full of visions of a better world and hope for the future and an eloquent expression of gratitude to the millions of voters who, across party affiliation and ideology, had rallied to his side over the past year and elevated him to this stunning victory. But most of all, it was a tribute to America: it spoke of a future filled with promise of what this country could and someday soon would be. The very best version of itself for all its citizens, and a beacon of hope for the world.

It was a magnificent speech, and no one else but Jack could have given it. Watching him speak so passionately to this enraptured crowd, she realized that however much their bond had strengthened over the past year and however close they might continue to become during the remainder of their days together, her husband would never belong to her again, at least not to her alone. She was struck suddenly by a memory of a quote about President Lincoln spoken after his death: "Now he belongs to the ages."

Jack was very much alive, thank God, and more animated and happier than she'd ever seen him. No one would be writing his epitaph tonight, when so much still lay ahead for him. But, she realized, there was something intangibly different about him now, a new aura that hadn't existed even a few hours ago. He wasn't just a politician or a leader or a man anymore: he was a legend.

Jack belongs to the ages now, too. Somehow, the thought was both poignant and bittersweet. He would never be solely hers again, if he ever had been. He belonged to the nation, to the world, and to history itself.

As her mind filled with these heady reflections, she could tell that the speech was winding down, that soon he'd be thanking everyone and walking offstage to begin the next chapter in his journey. But as it turned out, the surprises of the night weren't over quite yet. After Jack rattled off a string of thank-yous to his advisors, his supporters, and his family, she was shaken out of her reverie when she heard these words:

"And now, I want to thank the most important person of all, without whom this victory could not have happened and without whom I would not be standing where I am today. To my wife, Jacqueline—you deserve all the gratitude of our nation and all the thanks I can give you, for always standing by my side through the brightest and the darkest of days. I am so grateful to have you with me as we continue on this adventure for the next four years and beyond."

He turned from the podium, looked right into her eyes, and smiled at her. It was the same smile that had so enchanted her on the first night they'd met twelve years ago.

She heard the words, and for a moment she couldn't speak; she almost couldn't breathe. She dimly heard the people in the ballroom roaring their enthusiasm, celebrating her, but that meant nothing. What struck her to her very core was that her husband, who had long been so determined to preserve a certain degree of distance from her—who rarely even held her hand in public—was saying these words not merely to her but to the entire world. He was letting everyone know, without embarrassment or reticence, that he needed her. That she mattered. That he didn't care if the whole world knew this; that he *wanted* them to know.

Of course, there had been moments like this before, hints of his emotions shared carefully with the wider world when he spoke of her. His dedication to her in his book *Profiles in Courage*, which she had treasured more than she had ever let him know. And of course, his famous, amusing description of himself as "the man who accompanied Jacqueline Kennedy to Paris" during their trip in 1961.

But that had been different. As much as she appreciated his words and knew that he was genuinely proud of her accomplishments, she also sensed the traces of defensiveness, of preemption, in that remark. Wrapped up in the joke was a need to prove to the world that he was not threatened by her success, especially as it had been paired with one of his more disastrous first experiences as President after his meeting with Khrushchev in Vienna. He had made that charming, offhand remark less as a proud husband than as a leader determined to project to the world that it didn't matter if his wife upstaged him, that he was secure enough to celebrate her success. While others might have missed the undertone, she had not, and it left her uncertain how to feel about his words. So she had quickly banished them from her mind along with so much else he'd said and done over the course of their marriage. Best not to dwell on them too deeply, to avoid peeling back the layers of their true meaning. Back in those days, ignorance was, if not quite bliss, at least a way to survive and maintain their relationship as best she could.

But this was different. It couldn't have been clearer that this time he meant every word he was saying. All the events of the past year—their shared grief over Patrick's death; their reconnection after Dallas; all the slow, painstaking growth and deepening of their relationship since then—had been leading to this moment. And now that these words were out, hovering between them in the crackling air of this ballroom on election night, there was no taking them back. Nothing that happened in the future could erase what he'd just said to her in front of the entire world, on this magical night.

He loves me. And he wants the whole world to know.

She was shaken out of these dazzled thoughts by Caroline, who was pulling on her arm. "Mommy, Daddy wants us to come up there with him!"

Her daughter was right. She'd been so consumed with her own reflections that she hadn't even realized Jack was waving to her, inviting her and the children to join him onstage.

Still feeling dazed, she reached down and took both her children's hands and began walking up to the front of the stage. Jack had stepped down from the podium, and as they approached he took Caroline's hand as she ran to his left side and held out his other hand to her. She grasped it and squeezed hard, trying to express in that quick gesture all of her astounded love and pride. With John holding tightly to his mother's right hand, the four of them turned toward the cheering crowd as one unit: a new family portrait that would now live on forever as a part of American history.

Jack turned to her with a wink and a nod, and in one motion they lifted their entwined hands into the air, John and Caroline quickly picked up and copied the gesture, and the four of them stood there for what felt like both a second and an eternity, basking in the glow of the cheering crowd celebrating tonight's magnificent victory.

All too soon the magical moment was over, and the four of them dropped their arms as if on an unseen signal and began to wave at the throngs of supporters who were enraptured by the sight of the beautiful young first family celebrating this victory. The noise continued without ceasing, and she knew she'd have a headache very soon, but it didn't matter. All that mattered was that the four (soon to be five) of them were standing here together, savoring this moment. They'd lived through what seemed like everything the world could possibly throw at them over the past four years, and they had survived and come back stronger than they'd ever been before.

And then, in perhaps the most startling surprise of the night, her husband—who had long seemed almost allergic to any public displays of a romantic nature between them—wrapped his arm around her and pulled her to his side, waving to the cheering audience with his other hand. She closed her eyes and rested her head on his shoulder, wanting to shut out the noise of the ecstatic crowd and just to remember this precious moment that now belonged to the two of them forever. And suddenly, with a thousand flashing lightbulbs and cameras recording the image for posterity, she felt her face break into an ecstatic smile as Jack murmured a few words into her ear.

The next morning, when the pictures of the night's celebration appeared on the front pages of every newspaper around the world, the question on the minds of many readers wasn't about the details of the President's speech or his margin of victory or the political implications of this landslide re-election. The thing everyone in America most wanted to know—or so it seemed—was what had passed between the President and the First Lady in that brief moment. What had he said to make her smile so brilliantly, her face lit up so happily in front of the entire world?

No one would ever learn the answer to this tantalizing question. They kept the secret between themselves for the rest of their lives. But many years later, when she had to draw on her wells of strength to get through the challenges that lay ahead for them in the distant future, she would think back to this night and to the words he'd whispered to her in that moment: *This is all because of you. Not just tonight, but everything. Thank you, Jackie.*

It was the most beautiful, perfect moment of her life.

Chapter Four

Are you sure you'll be okay? I mean—is it going to happen today?"

She laughed, shaking her head. "I don't know, Jack. I can't predict the future."

"I know, but how do you feel? Do you think it *could* happen today?"

She rested her hand on her bulky stomach and shook her head. "I don't know. I don't think so. So, you should go about your business as planned until something changes."

She knew he had quite a bit of business to go about today. It had been two weeks since election night, and the glow of the victory celebration had almost immediately receded as the realities of planning a second administration became clear. She had heard him and Bobby debating potential choices for the new Cabinet late into last night: Should Dean Rusk stay or go as Secretary of State? Was it time for some new blood, or was it worth keeping him on for his experience and expertise? In addition to these questions, she knew he had a multitude of other decisions to make as he looked ahead to his second term.

But one even bigger question loomed large over everything else: *When would the new Kennedy baby make his or her debut?*

The press wanted to know. The country wanted to know. But most of all, it seemed, Jack wanted to know.

"I'm sorry to keep asking you. I just don't want to miss it. I want to be there this time."

She smiled and reached out across the breakfast table to take his hand. "Really, Jack, I feel fine. I don't think it's going to happen today, although honestly I wish it would, because I'm more than ready."

He nodded. "Okay. I'll be in the Oval with Bobby, but if anything happens . . ."

"I'll call you." She smiled. "Or if I'm otherwise occupied, I'll make sure that someone else does."

"Fair enough." He grinned, tossing aside his newspaper, and kissed her swiftly before standing up and walking out of the room.

"Good luck on the Rusk decision," she called after him as he departed.

"Oh—did you hear that?" He paused to look back at her, his face showing his embarrassment.

"You and Bobby aren't quiet when you talk about these kinds of things, Jack."

"Sorry we kept you awake. But I'll let you know how it turns out." He smiled again, then turned and strode out of the room.

The rest of the morning passed quietly. She puttered around the mansion for a bit before lying down on her bed and attempting to read the new book she'd started yesterday, but she couldn't concentrate on the words in front of her. The children were both at school, and she knew they'd be occupied with their friends for the next few hours. There was nothing for her to do, it seemed, but sit and wait for something to happen.

She gave up trying to rest, pulled herself off the bed, and began walking aimlessly down the corridors of the residence. She thought perhaps the motion would hasten the baby's arrival, but she felt no different as she slowly ambled along. Outside, she could see the last leaves falling off the trees through the window. Autumn was well underway, and soon winter and Christmas would arrive. Another November, another election, another baby—if all went well.

She impulsively decided to walk outside for a bit, to enjoy the slightly chilly air before the winter cold settled in. As she grabbed her coat and stepped out into the crisp fall sunshine, she looked up at the bright blue, nearly cloudless sky, almost dazzlingly bright. What a beautiful day this would be for a person to enter the world, she mused; for a new baby to be born.

All morning, she'd been fighting off memories of the last time; the hot summer day on which Patrick had been born, too soon and not yet ready for the world, in all its beauty and disarray. He had fought so bravely—or so Jack had told her afterward—but her baby son had slipped away before she'd ever gotten a chance to know him.

Remembering her lost baby boy, she stared up into the sunny sky, imagining God looking down on her as she sat outside the White House, the unparalleled symbol of power on earth at this moment in human history. Looking down with benign indifference, reminding her that none of that really meant anything at all. Being married to the most powerful man in the world didn't offer any protection against tragedy befalling her or their family. She'd learned that lesson the hard way, and in the aftermath of her grief over Patrick's death, her thoughts toward God had not been kind. Not that He had any right to complain. In those dark days after the loss of what she'd then thought would be her last child, she had reflected bitterly that should she ever manage to ascend to heaven and meet her maker, God would not like much of what she had to say to Him during their conversation.

But then Jack had been shot, and, of course, her angry resolve to dispense with God had quickly crumbled. In the backseat of the blood-stained limousine, in the hospital as she sat by her husband's side, holding his hand and silently begging him to keep his promise not to leave her, she had caved, and once again put aside her pride to beg God for His help. *Please, let him live. Don't take him from me and our children. Let us grow old together, let us see our children grow up. Please.*

And God had acceded to her tearful request, despite the previous bad blood between them. All might not be forgiven on her end (she wasn't a divinity, after all), but the two of them seemed to have reached a tentative détente. And yet for the past year, whenever she'd dutifully gone to church and sat with Jack and her children with her hands folded in prayer like the good Catholic she was presenting herself to the world as being, she felt less as if she were communing with her savior and more as if she were trying not to disturb a sleeping giant. She wanted nothing more from God at this point than to be left alone.

But now, as she gazed up at the brilliant sunny sky, she realized she wasn't free yet. There was still one more prayer she needed to send up to the heavens.

Please, let our baby arrive safely. Let him or her be healthy and happy, and live a good life. And if you do that—if you grant me this one last wish—I won't bother you anymore. And you can leave me alone for as long as you wish. Thirty, forty years more: whatever you see fit. Just give me that time with my husband and our children, and then I'll go quietly. But I can't endure another heartbreak . . . She paused, summoning her courage, *and really, you owe me this much. You know you do.*

The sun kept shining, the clouds swept across the sky, a few remaining leaves drifted gently down from the trees. Her dramatic inner monologue—half plea, half command—did not seem to be of much interest to God. Understandable, she supposed, as He had an entire universe to be getting on with, and no matter how famous she might be for this brief moment in history, ultimately she was just one of billions of people who were asking Him for this or that around the world. Like any parent, God surely got tired of it all after a while.

She gave up and slowly peeled herself off the hard bench she'd been sitting on, ready to continue her walk. But before she'd taken more than a few steps, the familiar stabbing pain told her that maybe, regardless of what she'd told her husband, today would be the day after all.

As she stepped back into the mansion, she paused for a moment and looked up at the sky and silently reiterated her desperate plea: *One more healthy baby. Just one more. Please.*

Twelve hours later, their little girl was born.

―――――――

"Can you look up for a moment, Mrs. Kennedy?"

The photographer's voice jerked her out of her reverie, and she pulled her eyes from her baby, with an apologetic smile. "Of course. I'm sorry."

"No need to apologize." The young woman reporter from *Vogue* smiled at her with understanding. "I imagine it's hard to take your eyes off of her for a second."

You have no idea, she thought to herself. "Yes, it is. But I'm sorry, I missed your last question—could you repeat it, please?"

It was four days before Christmas. The *Vogue* interview with the three children she'd agreed to months ago had been scheduled a week after she'd given birth to her daughter, almost as soon as she'd arrived home from the hospital.

In the past few days, she had been having second thoughts and had considered canceling more than once. But Jack had persuaded her it was best to go ahead. The country was insatiable for news about their new baby, and they'd have to share her with the world sooner or later. *Vogue* had promised to keep the interview brief, and she had already looked over the list of questions they planned to ask in advance of the reporter's arrival. A few quick queries, some practiced responses, and a couple new photos should satisfy the nation that the newest First Daughter had arrived safe and sound, and then she could forget about it until the article ran in a few months' time. Caroline and John would be joining them in a few moments for family photos, but the photographer had asked for a few shots of just her and the new baby first.

"Of course, Mrs. Kennedy. I asked about her name; it's so beautiful and unusual. I'm sure our readers would love to know how you and President Kennedy decided on it?"

She smiled, her first real smile since they'd sat down ten minutes earlier.

"Thank you. I was reading a book a few months ago while I was expecting, and I came across the name. We both thought it would be perfect."

This was mostly true, if not terribly detailed. Minimum information given with maximum politeness; that had been her motto since she'd moved into the White House four years earlier, and she saw no reason to adjust her habits now.

But of course, there'd been a bit more to it than that.

"She's beautiful, isn't she?" she had whispered to Jack, as they gazed down at their daughter for the first time a month ago.

"Perfection." He reached out and touched the baby's tiny fist, and she wrapped her little hand around his finger, yawning and looking totally unimpressed at having the President of the United States as her father. But she was healthy and had seemed happy since her arrival into the world a few hours earlier, and nothing else mattered.

He turned and smiled at her. "And you—you were amazing."

She smiled back. "It wasn't so hard." This was true; it had been the easiest delivery she'd ever had. And now that their daughter was here, safe in her arms, her anxiety felt like a distant memory. Finally, after nearly a year of constant worry and fear, she felt at peace.

"You never give yourself enough credit, Jackie. You made it look easy, but that doesn't mean it was. And honestly, after this I really think there's nothing in the world you can't do."

She smiled, reveling in the warmth she felt at his admiration. After all these years, making her husband proud still filled her with a certain glow that no other achievement could replicate.

And he knew exactly what he was talking about this time. He had rushed to her hospital room as soon as he'd gotten the news she had gone into labor, and for the next few hours he hadn't left her side. He'd stayed with her through the whole delivery, holding her hand and encouraging her, and when their daughter had arrived at last, she saw the same tears of joy in his eyes that she felt prickling in her own.

It was hard to believe that just a year and three months ago, they'd come together in a similar hospital room and shed tears over the loss of baby Patrick. Patrick's death had broken both of them, but while the pain of that loss would never fully heal, it had brought them closer in a way they hadn't been before during the turbulent decade of their marriage. The past year had been filled with so many different emotions: grief for their lost child, the fear of losing Jack forever on that horrible day in Dallas, then hope, and finally pure joy at the arrival of their beautiful, healthy baby. She felt as if they'd traveled a lifetime together in barely a years' time, not knowing what their final destination would be, only that they would arrive there together.

And now they were here at last, holding their baby girl, and everything was perfect. She was perfect.

"So," Jack's words shook her out of her contemplations, "are we ready to pick a name for this little angel?"

"Well, we already have a middle name, don't we? Or two names—since we can't choose just one."

He nodded. They'd avoided picking a first name before the baby's arrival, perhaps out of superstition or simply dread of the worst-case scenario, but they'd already agreed the baby would be given the names of both of her Kennedy grandparents.

"Which leaves us with one more decision to make. Any ideas?"

She nodded. Although she had done some research and come up with a girl's name a few months ago, she had refrained from sharing it until now just in case.

"I was thinking of Aurora. It means sunrise, or dawn—it feels appropriate, wouldn't you say?"

He nodded. "Yes, I would. And it's a beautiful name. I think it suits her: she looks like an Aurora, don't you think?"

She laughed. "I'm not sure what that looks like, but I do love the name. I thought we should pick something pretty, but unique . . . and also . . ." She broke off suddenly.

He reached out and gently touched her face, turning her to look at him. "Jackie?"

She pulled herself together, then looked into his eyes. "It's a little bit like Arabella—but not too close. I thought it would be, I don't know, sort of a way to remember." She stopped talking, feeling the tears begin to well up and not wanting to spoil this moment by letting them fall. "I don't want us to ever forget her, Jack."

He was silent, his head bowed, and when he looked up at her she thought she saw a tear in the corner of his own eye, though it might have been a trick of the room's light or simply her physical exhaustion after all that had happened that day. Then he reached over and took her hand.

"We won't. We won't ever forget—not for as long as we live."

She nodded silently, then glanced back at their baby, whose eyes were now closed as though her parents' conversation had ceased to hold her interest. "Well, then, that's settled."

"Yes. Welcome to the world, Aurora Rose Josephine Kennedy."

And while their daughter remained asleep and oblivious to the significance of the moment, they smiled down together at their perfect, healthy baby—their new dawn.

Part Two

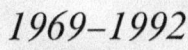

The Middle

1969–1992

Chapter Five

The White House
January 19, 1969

The small, dark-haired girl sat in the middle of the room, surrounded by dolls and books and stuffed animals strewn around haphazardly, looking both sad and confused as she tried again to make sense of the situation in which she found herself.

"But mommy, I don't understand. Why do we have to leave?"

She knelt down beside her daughter, sweeping a stray dark curl off of her forehead, and tried again to explain.

"Today is our last day in this house, baby. Tomorrow, we're moving to our new house. Remember, we went out there last week? You saw the big yard, and the stables, and your new bedroom?"

"Yes," the little girl nodded, her forehead crinkling as she remembered the house she'd skipped happily through just a few days ago. "But why do we have to leave *this* house, Mommy? Why do we have to leave our home?"

She had explained this all before, but clearly it wasn't sticking. How did you explain to a four-year-old why they had to leave the only home they've ever known? She pulled her daughter into her arms, and the little girl snuggled up against her, looking into her mother's face for anything that might help her make sense of her world being turned upside down.

"Aurora," she began, "do you remember how we talked about your daddy's job? What he does when he goes to work every day?"

The girl nodded. "Yes. Daddy is the President of the United States." She spoke the title carefully, and with pride.

"That's right. And you know what an important job that is, right? How he does things every single day that help people around the country, and even the whole world?"

"Yes," she nodded, though in truth this was still a bit too big a concept for her to wrap her mind around. But her father's job was important; that much she did understand.

"Well, it's a very big job. And very special. In fact, it's so big and so special that just one person can't do it forever. People have to take turns."

"Like when we play games at school?"

"That's right. Everyone needs to have a turn. It's the same with being president. One person can't do it forever; that wouldn't be fair, would it?" *In more ways than one,* she thought.

"No," Aurora agreed, shaking her head. "But Daddy is very good at his job, right, Mommy?"

"Yes, baby. He's very good at it."

"Well, then, I think they should let him keep doing it. Since he's so good."

She smiled down at her younger daughter. "Well, no matter how good he is, there are rules in our country, honey. One person can be president for eight years, and then someone else gets a turn. Daddy has had his job for eight years, so now it's time for someone else to get to try it."

"Mr. Nixon?" She'd heard the name mentioned in conversations around the dinner table as they planned their family's move.

"That's right. Mr. Nixon will be the new president, starting tomorrow. And he and his wife and their family will move into this house, because that's part of the job. Every president gets to live in the White House."

"But Mommy, maybe they'll let us stay here? And let us keep our rooms? If we asked them?" Flush with excitement at her discovery of this potential loophole, she gave her mother her most heart-melting smile.

But her mother only laughed, with a twinge of sadness in her voice. "Sorry, baby, but no. We can't stay here once the Nixons move in. It will become their house, but do you know who it really belongs to?"

This was too much for the little girl to take in. The house she'd always thought of as her own, which was now being moved in to by the strange Nixons, had another owner? "Who?"

"It belongs to the American people. All of us. Every single person who lives in America is the real owner of this house, Aurora. That's why we have to leave. While your daddy was president, we got to live here, and it was an honor; we were very lucky. But now he has to let Mr. Nixon have his turn as president, so we have to move out of this house. But in a way, it will always belong to us, because we're Americans. Do you understand?"

She didn't, not really. These lofty ideas were difficult for even a very bright preschooler to grasp (and as her parents and teachers could attest, she *was* very bright). But even if the words didn't quite make sense to her yet, she could see that resistance to her fate was futile. Tomorrow, they were leaving the house she'd grown up in and loved and moving to a strange new place. She'd failed to persuade either her mother or father to change their minds, and now she was beginning to think that this decision about their family's future had been made by a mysterious force even more powerful than her parents. Clearly, arguing was not going to get her anywhere. There was nothing more to be done.

As she tried to absorb this strange twist of fate, the biggest shock of her young life, her mother said something that would remain sharply etched in her mind for decades to come, even if she couldn't fully understand it yet.

"I know you're sad to leave this house, Aurora. I think we're all a little bit sad. But we're going to make lots of great memories in our new house. We'll have so much fun there. And you, me, Daddy, Caroline, and John will all be together. And that's the most important thing of all—that our family is together, wherever we may be."

She nodded; that much she could understand. "Okay, mommy. But I can take all my toys with me to the new house, can't I?"

"Of course you can, baby. Just put them into these boxes, and tomorrow the moving men will take them to our new house and put them in your brand-new bedroom."

She smiled, kissed her daughter on the top of her head, and stood up and walked out of her room.

She strode into the nearly empty sitting area in the family quarters and sat down on the one remaining couch, looking weary. "Well, I guess that went about as well as it could have."

"She's still sad about moving out?"

"Sad, confused, maybe a little worried. But she took it well in the end, once I explained it all to her. Or tried to."

He extinguished his cigar and looked at her ruefully. "Well, then, our daughter may be handling this whole thing better than me."

"Don't be ridiculous, Jack. You've done everything you can to help him, to ease the transition." She was proud of the grace her husband had shown in welcoming his successor— and one-time friend, colleague, and presidential rival—into his new role. But it was still so strange to think that in just a day's time, Richard and Pat Nixon would be sitting in this room, in the mansion that would be theirs at last.

"President Nixon," he sighed, shaking his head ruefully. "That will take some getting used to, huh?"

She nodded with a slightly wistful smile. "I suspect it will." She leaned towards him, her long dark hair tumbling forward as she swept a few strands off her forehead. "But we'll be moving on to new adventures ourselves. This isn't the end, Jack; it's a new beginning."

He nodded. He knew she was right, but it still didn't erase the strangeness of this moment. Somehow, when he'd run for president, when he'd won the office twice, he'd never really considered what would happen at the end of his eight years in the White House. It had seemed so far away that it wasn't even worth thinking about. He'd always lived in the moment, never really expecting his life to be long and wanting to seize every moment while it was happening rather than thinking about what he'd do when his presidency ended.

And now, before he could even absorb the remarkable highs and lows of the past decade of his life, it was almost over. Tomorrow, he'd be a fifty-one-year-old ex-President with the rest of his life ahead of him and—if he was honest with himself—no idea what to do with it.

"Honestly," she said, breaking into his musings, "aren't you a little curious about what life will be like when we leave here? Getting to be a normal family, with the freedom to do anything we want whenever we want to? And with all the burdens of this—" she made a sweeping gesture around the magnificent room they were sitting in, one of many she'd lovingly restored during the early years they'd spent here—"off your shoulders forever?"

He smiled slightly, for she did have a point. After tomorrow, life would never be the same for him or any of their family, but it was also true that in twenty-four hours, America's troubles would officially be Richard Nixon's problem.

1968 had not been an easy year for him or for the country.

It had started well enough. On New Year's Eve 1967, they'd held a magnificent party at the White House to welcome in the new year. "It's the last full year of your presidency," Jackie had pointed out as she meticulously planned the celebration for weeks in advance. "We have to start it off right." And, as with every other event she'd hosted as First Lady, it had indeed been a night to remember.

As the final year of his presidency began, he'd been too busy to focus much on the past, but every now and then he did pause to reflect on the events of the previous three years. His second term had proven as eventful as his first, if not more so. In 1964, he'd finally signed the Civil Rights Act, enshrining into law the long-delayed promise of America for all its citizens. A few months after his swearing-in in 1965, he'd signed legislation creating the Medicare program. And in 1967 the last American troops had left Vietnam, and he and Leonid Brezhnev had signed a new, far-reaching peace treaty between the United States and the Soviet Union. The Cold War wasn't over, but it had definitely thawed, and he felt gratified that the world he was passing onto his children would be safer than the one he and his generation had inherited. And because of his efforts, he'd been awarded the Nobel Peace Prize that year. Heading into 1968, the future seemed filled with hope.

But the global peace he'd worked so hard to build during his presidency was not matched by a similar peace within the country's borders. In April of 1968, Martin Luther King, Jr. was assassinated, and the country reeled in shock as violent protests erupted and cities around the nation went up in flames.

Suddenly, it seemed everyone was angry. Black Americans were angry that after all this time and after the much-vaunted Civil Rights Act they'd fought so hard for was officially the law of the land, the scourges of violence and racism continued to live on in the country. And many southern whites were equally angry at him and at anyone who supported the civil rights movement, which for reasons he could never understand, far too many of them viewed as a threat to themselves.

Meanwhile against this dark backdrop, the 1968 presidential election unfolded. The two most obvious candidates, his brother and his vice-president, had both opted out. Lyndon was getting older, his health was failing, and he decided against trying to win the country's greatest political office for himself after eight years of serving in the background. Bobby had considered making his own run, especially once word was out that Lyndon wouldn't be a candidate, but ultimately, he had decided against it as well.

"It's too soon," he had counseled his brother. "The country has had eight years of Kennedys in office, and if you run now, they may hold that against you. They'll want something new and different. I think you're better off waiting a few years before making your own run. And when you decide the time is right, you know I'll do everything possible to help you get here."

Bobby had agreed with his advice, though he had admitted he sometimes felt pangs of regret at his decision.

Instead, he had thrown his hat into the ring for the open Senate seat from New York State, and defying predictions and carpetbagger accusations, he'd won the race handily. He and Ted would serve in the Senate together next year, and the youngest brother would be able to claim with pride that he'd gotten to the job first.

With the two most obvious candidates passing up a run, the Democratic Party had settled on Hubert Humphrey, the senator from Minnesota, as its presidential nominee, while the Republicans again chose Richard Nixon. At first, he had been convinced that his old rival was doomed to fail again, but as the year progressed, his assessment of the race began to change. People were in a foul mood, the country felt unsettled, and suddenly, it seemed more likely than not that voters might opt for a completely different path in November.

Of course, he'd intended to do all he could to help Humphrey in the campaign. He was well positioned to do so; despite all the turmoil swirling through the nation, his own approval rating remained steadily in the high sixties. As he wrapped up his final few months in office, his plan was to hit the campaign trail in earnest, beginning in September, to help bring the presidency home for the Democrats one last time.

And then, in late August, Jackie told him they needed to talk.

It was a few days after the Democratic convention. They were on vacation in Hyannis Port, taking a break from the beastly heat and general unpleasantness of Washington in late summer. One day, after the kids had finished swimming in the ocean and were busy playing with their cousins, Jackie had pulled him aside before dinnertime to take a walk on the beach, just the two of them. It was one of the first times they'd been alone together amidst the chaos of the extended family gathering, and he could tell that she had something important on her mind.

As they strolled along the beach together, she watched the waves crash against the sand, not saying anything for a moment, then turned to him, her eyes as serious as he'd ever seen them.

"Jack—I have to tell you something."

"What is it?" She looked nervous, as though she were having a hard time forming the right words.

She hesitated for a moment, then said it: "I don't want you to campaign this fall."

He was startled enough to stop in his tracks, staring at her. She'd never said anything like this before—not after Dallas, not even during the 1964 campaign. "Why not, Jackie?"

"You know why not." She stopped walking for a moment and stared out to sea, then turned to him looking resolute.

"Is this about Martin Luther King?" They'd attended the funeral together just four months ago; Coretta, Martin's widow, had asked him to speak. Watching her in the audience as he gave his eulogy, he'd caught the same look on Jackie's face then that he saw there now—a strange combination of emotions, both resolutely determined and terribly afraid.

"Yes, but it's not just that. What happened to him nearly happened to you. And it still could."

He shook his head. "No. We'll have the Secret Service there; they'll take every precaution. You don't have to worry . . ."

"Oh, really? Don't I? Because I'm pretty sure the Secret Service was there in Dallas, and yet you still got shot and nearly killed. And now, it's even worse. This country's gone insane, Jack. The violence, the hatred: there's so much hate in America right now. I don't want you to put yourself out there in the middle of it and risk your life."

She was glaring at him, and he saw the same fierce, determined expression on her face that she'd had in the hospital room in Dallas nearly five years ago. She was as serious as he'd ever seen her—and she wasn't done yet.

"Do you know that I've had nightmares ever since that day, Jack? I still can't sleep sometimes. I close my eyes, and I see the bullet hitting you and you falling over into my lap . . ." She broke off, turned away for a moment, and when she whipped back towards him, he could see the tears staining her face even as she tried to ignore them.

"Listen to me, Jackie . . ." He reached out and touched her arm, but she pulled it away. She was as upset as he had ever seen her.

"No, Jack, I want *you* to listen, because this is the most important thing I've ever said to you. I will *not* lose you. Do you understand? I won't. It's not an option. I don't care what promises you have to break; I don't care how much you have to disappoint Hubert Humphrey or the Democratic Party or the entire damn country. I will not sit back and let you put yourself in danger to win an election for someone else. It's not worth it. Nothing is worth losing you; nothing is worth the children and I spending the rest of our lives without you. That cannot happen. I can't live through it. I won't survive."

She was crying now, the tears streaming down her face, and he was stunned. She had never spoken to him like this before, never laid open her feelings so bare and raw. She'd always stood by his side, smiled, waved, told him she'd support him no matter what, even after she'd watched him nearly die that day in Dallas. She's been so brave and stoic for so long, he'd always taken her strength and composure for granted, he realized now. But it was clear she'd reached her breaking point, and she wasn't about to budge on this.

Nearly five years ago, he had almost died in his wife's arms. He still remembered his last thoughts before fading into blackness in the back of the car: first, that if he died, he'd never get to see his children grow up. And second, that he had let her down, over and over. He'd never been the husband she deserved, the man she thought she'd married. The man he should have been.

The next day in the hospital, when they'd talked about the past and the future, he'd promised her things would be different. *I'll never hurt you again.* What he had meant, of course, was that he would put a stop to his infidelities—and he had, from that day forward. He'd kept his promise to her.

But as he looked at his wife now, watching her tears fall and hearing the anger in her voice, he realized that it wasn't only his betrayals of her and their marriage vows that had the ability to cause her pain. If he went out to campaign for Humphrey, he would be putting himself at risk. Even if the odds were that everything would be fine, she had every reason to worry. He had barely escaped being murdered right before her eyes. And he realized now, for the first time, how hard those memories must have been for her to live with for the past five years. Because things had ended happily, he had convinced himself all was well and pushed down his own fears in order to move forward with his life and his presidency the only way he knew how. They'd never really talked about that day, and he'd assumed that like him, she wanted only to leave it behind them as they tried to begin their lives anew.

But now he realized how naïve that hope had been. Five years later, his wife was still having nightmares about the day he had nearly been assassinated. He knew that there was no way he could risk putting her through that kind of pain again. Even if nothing happened to him, making her constantly live in fear while he took unnecessary risks was too much to ask of her. He couldn't do it. She had been through so much in the fifteen years of their marriage, and too much of it had been his fault. He couldn't do anything that would hurt her that much ever again.

"Jackie." She'd turned away from him again, staring back at the sea, and he could see her trying to wipe away her tears. He reached out and touched her shoulder gently, and she turned around to face him.

"I'm sorry. You're right. I won't do it."

She looked at him with amazement, and her expression caused him another twinge of remorse. Was she surprised that he'd agreed so quickly? Had she thought he would refuse, that he would be willing to ignore her feelings and let her stew in her anxiety and fear while he traveled the country, exposing himself to crowds and danger and risking his life again?

"You won't?"

"Of course not. Not if it's going to make you feel this way. And not if there's any possibility that something could happen. I won't risk it, for you and the kids. I won't take that chance. You're right; it's not worth it."

She stared into his eyes for a moment, as if trying to figure out if he was serious, then deciding that he was. She smiled at him haltingly, and he reached out and pushed back a strand of her hair that the wind had blown into her eyes. "Thank you."

"No, don't. Don't thank me. Just tell me—why didn't you say anything about this before, during the last election?"

"That was different." She shook her head. "You were running for reelection, and I knew how badly you wanted to win and how much the country needed you to win. I wasn't going to ask you not to run again when it was so important. But this— you don't need to do this."

"No." He lifted her chin up and looked into her eyes again. "Did you worry this much back then, the whole time I was campaigning? And not say anything to me about it?"

She looked away and didn't reply, but her silence gave him his answer. He wrapped his arms around her and pulled her against him. "I never realized . . . I never knew you felt this way."

"It's not your fault."

"It is. I should have known. We should have talked more about everything, after Dallas. I'm sorry I made you go through all that alone."

She looked up, shaking her head. "It's not your fault, Jack. I didn't want to worry you. And I guess . . . maybe I didn't want to think about it either. To admit to myself just how scared I was."

"Well, from now on, I think we need a new rule in our marriage."

She smiled, and even laughed a little as she said, "I didn't realize we had old rules."

"You know what I mean. You're the strongest person I've ever known, Jackie, but that doesn't mean you should have to keep everything inside. If you're upset or worried or afraid, I want you to tell me. That's what I'm supposed to be here for."

She smiled more broadly, shaking her head in wonder. "You know—sometimes I don't even recognize you anymore, Jack. After everything that's happened these past few years, I mean. But I like these new rules of yours. From now on I'll tell you everything, I promise."

He nodded. "So that's settled. I won't campaign this year. But you'll have to tell Hubert Humphrey. I'm pretty sure he likes you better than he likes me, anyway."

She laughed, and, wrapping their arms around one another, they began walking back to the house together.

And so as autumn arrived and the presidential campaign headed into the homestretch, he told Humphrey he wouldn't be able to join him on the trail. No rallies, no motorcades. No places where there was any possibility someone might be lurking with a gun, waiting to end his life.

He did what he could behind the scenes; attended fundraisers, a few small gatherings, even appeared in a few campaign ads to urge Americans to vote for the Democratic ticket. But as Election Day drew nearer, he could see that the tide was turning.

Election Night 1968 was as different as possible from 1964. The kids went to bed at their normal bedtime after wishing their Uncle Bobby good luck in his Senate race. He, Jackie, Bobby, Ethel, Ted, Joan, and the rest of his family along with a handful of their friends gathered around the TV in the White House, watching as the results came in.

Bobby's victory was the highlight of the night, but everything pretty much went downhill after the New York Senate race was called. By 11 pm, the verdict was in: Richard Nixon had narrowly defeated both Humphrey and third-party candidate George Wallace to become the next President of the United States.

"Well, that's that," he said, pulling himself to his feet, feeling far more exhausted than he had on that last exhilarating election night four years ago, though this time he'd done nothing more than sit and stare at the television for the last few hours. He snapped off the TV, and slowly the group disbanded until only he and Jackie were left.

"I'm sorry, Jack," she said quietly. "I know this isn't what you were hoping for."

"It's all right." He sighed.

"President Nixon," she said, shaking her head.

"Well—I guess we should be glad we didn't have to call him that for the last eight years, right?"

She smiled. "There's the silver lining. Come on, I'm exhausted. Let's go to bed."

———

The next day, the recriminations began. Why had Humphrey lost? Who was to blame?

Should JFK have done more to help Humphrey?

Why didn't he go out and campaign with him?

Wouldn't he have fought harder to help his brother win, if Bobby had decided to run?

Is that why he stayed at home, because with Bobby out of the race, he didn't care enough about the party, about America, about its future?

He ignored the criticisms he knew people were muttering behind his back. There was nothing to be gained by addressing them. He met with Nixon a few days later, smiled and clasped hands with his former rival for the cameras and talked with him for hours about foreign and domestic policy, doing all he could to help him ease into his presidency. It was a hard job, and no one except the men who'd done it could really understand how hard. And like it or not, Richard Nixon would soon be part of that exclusive club. He wanted him to succeed, or at least not fail spectacularly, for the sake of the country that he'd served for his entire adult life.

As his last days in the White House ticked down, he occasionally wondered, idly, if it would have made a difference if he'd gone out to campaign. But it was an unanswerable question, something that could only be known in an alternative universe where he had made different choices. In this one, he'd made the only choice that was possible for him: to honor the promise he had made five years ago not to hurt his wife again. Keeping himself alive for Jackie and their children was as important as anything he'd ever done as president. And sparing her pain, anxiety, and fear was worth any price he had to pay.

Even if that meant four years of Richard Nixon in the White House.

———————

Before he knew it, the next morning had arrived—his last morning as President of the United States.

He awoke early, his back pain flaring again, but he tried studiously to ignore it so he could focus on these last hours of this momentous eight-year period of his life.

He walked into the dining room in the family residence and was surprised to find he wasn't the first member of the family awake on this final morning.

"Hi, Buttons," he smiled at his older daughter, who was sitting at the table eating cereal and drinking a glass of orange juice. "You're up early today."

Caroline smiled at him. "I couldn't sleep, so I decided to get up and have breakfast. It's going to be a long day, isn't it?"

"Yes, it will—we'll go to the inauguration in a few hours, then back here to collect our bags, and off we go." He sat down, mulling over all the changes that were about to happen for him, Jackie, and their children. After today, nothing would ever be quite the same again for any of them.

Caroline nodded, looking thoughtful. "Dad, can I ask you something?"

"Of course. What is it, honey?"

She paused, looked down for a minute and then back up at him. "What are you going to do now?"

"What do you mean?"

"I mean—you've been president for eight years. That's a long time. It's almost my whole life. I don't even remember anything much before we moved into this house, before you were elected the first time. And now you have to leave it behind, and do something else . . ." She paused, looking intently at her father. "Do you know what you're going to do next?"

He shook his head ruefully. "No, I can't say that I do. But I'll figure it out." He looked at her closely, trying to assess her expression in the early morning light. "And what about you? I mean, we've lived in the White House since you were three. How do you feel about leaving all of this behind?"

She smiled a bit wistfully and responded thoughtfully. "I'll be okay, Dad. We all will. I mean sure, it will be weird leaving this house after all the years we've spent here, but it's like Mom always told us: the White House was never going to be our home forever. John and I have always known that. And Aurora—well, she's still so little, but she's smart, and I think she's starting to understand that, too." She nodded sagely, looking, as she so often did, wise beyond her eleven years. "We'll all be okay, Dad. I just want to make sure you will be too."

He smiled at her, touched by her concern, and knew that he couldn't let her worry about him this way. Somehow he'd have to figure things out.

"Don't worry about me. I promise I'll be okay, Buttons."

She smiled, and he thought he saw his first glimpse of her future teenage self as she rolled her eyes slightly at him. "Dad, are you really going to call me that forever? I mean, I'm almost twelve years old now."

"Sorry, honey. Sometimes I forget. So I may just end up calling you Buttons until you're fifty—you don't mind, do you?"

She laughed, shaking her head. "I guess it's all right. Just not in front of anyone else, okay?"

"Okay, honey. I promise."

They smiled at one another, and he was glad that he and his daughter had had time for this final talk before the rest of this portentous day began. And he realized that even if he couldn't quite answer her question yet, he'd have to figure it out soon for her, John's, Aurora's, and Jackie's sakes.

The rest of the morning sped by in a surreal blur. He tried to take in all the final moments of his last morning in the White House, but time was moving too fast. Before he knew it, Nixon's inauguration was over, and he had walked out of the White House for the last time with his family by his side as they headed off to what Jackie had described as their next adventure. He hoped she was right, because he couldn't see it yet. In fact, he realized that for the first time in decades he had absolutely no idea what tomorrow would hold, and that was deeply unsettling.

But this was his very last moment as president; he couldn't let his sadness or gloom show. He wanted to leave office on the highest note possible to close out these extraordinary eight years.

As the family walked together toward the helicopter that would chopper them to their new house in the Virginia countryside, he took Aurora's hand. She was skipping towards the plane, looking excited for the ride ahead, and he wondered if she fully understood what this final departure from the home she'd grown up in really meant.

"Daddy," she said, "are you sad to leave?"

He smiled at her and ruffled her dark hair. "Maybe a little bit, honey. How about you?"

"I was," his daughter replied. "But I'm not anymore. Because Mommy told me that the important thing is that wherever we live, we'll have lots of fun, and we'll all be together. So now I'm not sad anymore."

He nodded. "Mommy is very smart."

As they reached the helicopter, he turned to Jackie, Caroline, and John—how much they'd grown since they'd moved into this house eight years ago! —and said, "One last wave for the cameras, everyone?"

And the five of them turned toward the slew of photographers recording their final departure from the White

House, smiling and waving in their very last moment as America's First Family.

As this image flashed across TV screens around the nation, Walter Cronkite's voice intoned, "And that's the end of the Kennedy family's time in the White House. It's certainly been an eventful eight years. It will be quite interesting to see what they decide to do next. And now, let's go to President Nixon's inaugural address . . ."

A quick fade out of history from one era to another.

But as the now-former First Lady had predicted, the next adventure was just about to begin.

Chapter Six

S he sat cross-legged on the couch in the living room, the sunlight pouring in from the open window on this beautiful spring day and lighting up her face as she checked off her list and talked through her plans.

"I think about a week in London, then onto Paris for another week or so. Maybe a few days on the French Riviera, then Italy and Greece. Maybe we should take the kids to see the Roman ruins and the Acropolis; Caroline and John are old enough to appreciate those now, I think, and they've been studying them in school . . ."

Her enthusiasm was contagious, and her husband couldn't help smiling as she ran down her list of potential stops on their upcoming vacation. It was the first time she'd seen him smile in weeks, which made her both happy and a bit worried.

"What do you think, Jack?"

"I think it sounds fine." He shifted in his chair, stubbing out his cigar and wishing he could summon a bit more enthusiasm for this trip, or for anything else.

She looked up from her notepad to gaze at him. "What's wrong? Did I miss something?"

"No, it all sounds great. It's a lot to pack into a month, though."

"It'll be fine." She waved her hand, looking unconcerned. "Remember, we don't have any official state duties to attend to, so we can spend all our time seeing the sights and enjoying Europe like a normal family on vacation."

She'd been waiting for this moment for years. Since the day Jack had been sworn in for his second term she'd been silently counting down the days and months in her head as she looked forward to this trip. Of course, traveling the world as President and First Lady was an honor, and they'd had many extraordinary experiences during their eight years in the White House. But this trip was different; not a single state visit or formal dinner or parade on the agenda, just time together as a family to wander through cobblestone streets and swim in the ocean and picnic by the Seine or do whatever they might decide to do on a whim. No one could stop them from doing as they pleased anymore, now that their time at 1600 Pennsylvania Avenue was consigned to the history books. For the first time ever, her family of five would take a European vacation that was just for *them*.

"That sounds great, Jackie."

She regarded him seriously, the glow of a moment before leaving her face. "You don't sound very happy about any of it."

"No, I am. I know how much this means to you. We'll have fun."

She shook her head. "You don't seem very convinced of that. And I know it's not because I haven't done my very best to sell you on this trip for the past few weeks, so tell me, what's going on? Do you not want to go?"

"Of course I do."

"Then what is it? What's bothering you?"

"Nothing."

"Jack, stop it." She rose from the couch and walked over to sit down next to him. "I can always tell when you're lying, you know."

He sighed. Of course she could. And she'd had far too much experience at it. But this wasn't a lie, exactly; he just wasn't sure how to describe his feelings, even to himself.

"I think the trip sounds great. Really, Jackie. You've done an amazing job planning everything, and I'm sure it'll be fantastic. That's not what this is about."

"Then what?"

He shrugged. How to begin to explain it to her? He turned the dead cigar over in his fingers idly as he tried to come up with words that would explain his frame of mind.

"The thing is, I don't know what to do after it's over."

"Once we get back home?"

"Yes. And for the rest of the summer and the rest of the year . . ."

For the rest of my life.

It had been four months since they'd left the White House and begun their new life. Or rather, she and the children had begun new lives. He wasn't quite sure what, if anything, he could be said to have accomplished this year after handing the presidency over to Richard Nixon.

They had settled into their new house in the Virginia countryside back in January after Jackie had discovered and fallen in love with it the previous fall. They'd decided to sell their country house Wexford after five years to move into a bigger permanent home, and this new place certainly fit the bill. It was spacious, sprawling even, with eight bedrooms, extensive grounds, a swimming pool, and stables for his wife's and daughters' horses.

From the moment they'd left the White House and moved into their new home, Jackie had thrived like a plant in sunlight. She was more relaxed than she had been in years, to the point where she seemed almost to glow with happiness and contentment. She spent her days riding horses, reading books, playing with the children—she had even begun teaching Aurora how to ride.

He knew that part of her newfound serenity was because she loved the house itself, but he could only imagine that much of her exuberance was a result of leaving the White House behind. Not that she hadn't been happy there; as she had pointed out to him rather wistfully when they were preparing to depart, some of the happiest moments of their marriage had occurred during the past eight years. But now she was finally free of the burden that he had belatedly realized she'd carried with her ever since Dallas: the daily fear that some other terrible thing would happen to him and shatter her life to pieces. After five years of living with that nightmare scenario always in the back of her mind, the relative safety and calmness of the Virginia countryside must feel like a gift. He could hardly blame her for being relieved to leave that fear behind her.

All three children had taken to their new lives quickly as well. If Caroline and John ever missed the White House, they gave no sign of it. They were attending a local private school, busy with friends and studying and sports, and every morning when the five of them ate breakfast together—one of the best parts of retirement, he had to admit—they were full of chatter and plans for the day, not seeming to be troubled at all by nostalgia for their old life as presidential offspring. Aurora, meanwhile, was about to begin kindergarten in the fall, and so excited about learning to read picture books and her new pony that her parents had given her a few months ago that she could hardly talk about anything else. The Kennedy family, it seemed, was thriving in their post-White House existence.

The only exception, as it turned out, was him.

The truth was, now that his presidency was over, he didn't know what to do with himself. He woke up early almost every morning, out of habit, then realized he had no meetings, no appointments, nothing whatever to fill his day. He ambled around the house, read every newspaper from cover to cover, walked around the expansive yard every morning and afternoon before returning to the house to watch the evening news, keeping vague tabs on what was happening in the country he'd so recently led and in the world he'd helped shape up until a few months ago.

He knew he had plenty to be grateful for, and tried hard to remind himself of this when his newfound restlessness and gloom began to dominate his thoughts in the first few months after leaving the White House. He should have known this was coming, he realized now; he should have made more plans for his post-presidential life. Maybe he'd been in denial that it was all about to come to an end, or maybe he just hadn't wanted to face that fact. But now, there were times when he felt as though the monotony of his new existence would consume him.

In the old days, he might have filled the empty spaces in his life with a distraction in the form of a new romantic dalliance—*what Jackie doesn't know can't hurt her*, he used to tell himself, knowing even then that it was a lie, but unable to stop himself from going down that path again and again, whenever he faced temptation. But those days were long gone. Dallas had changed all of that for him, and he could honestly say that he had no regrets about committing fully to his marriage at last, after everything he and Jackie had been through together. And it wasn't that type of distraction he was looking for now, anyway. He didn't want a temporary rush of adrenaline; he just wanted to feel like his life once again had some larger purpose, now that he'd managed to survive long enough to join the ex-presidents' club.

He had thought at first that the major benefit of his very early retirement was that he'd be able to spend more time with his children. And he had truly enjoyed watching Caroline ride horses with her mother, helping John with his school projects, listening to Aurora's increasing progress at spelling and reading (she was clearly destined to be a lover of books like Jackie and himself).

However, after a few months of this, his children staged an intervention.

"Dad," Caroline had said one evening after dinner back in April when he'd offered to come to her tennis match after school the next day to watch her play, "We really appreciate that you want to spend so much time with us. But maybe it's okay if you skip some things."

"We think maybe you need to find some other stuff to do besides hanging out with us," John interjected helpfully.

"Thanks," he replied, feeling a bit stung. Caroline came up to him and put her arm around him.

"Dad, don't get us wrong. We love that you're home more now, but every time you come to any of our games and school things the Secret Service has to come too, and then everyone looks at you the whole time, and it gets so weird."

"We think maybe you should spend more time with other grownups," John added. "Besides just Mom and Uncle Bobby."

His son had a point. He'd barely seen any of his old friends over the past few months. He'd been so busy trying to adjust to his new life that he'd neglected many of the people who'd been part of his old one.

"And maybe you should find a new hobby," Caroline piped up. "Something different that'll take your mind off politics for a while. Mom said you used to paint once; maybe you could try that again?"

"Or you could learn to fly a helicopter, and I could take lessons too?" John asked hopefully.

He smiled. "I don't think your mother would like that idea, John. And I was never much of a painter. But you may be on to something. Maybe I do need a hobby."

He mulled this idea over during the next few weeks, but nothing much appealed to him. He didn't want to simply find some pointless activity to fill his days. For eight years he'd been President of the United States. How exactly did you follow that up? How could he move forward with his life when it felt as though he'd already peaked before the age of fifty?

These questions kept him up at night, the way worries about foreign policy and nuclear war used to. Even his worries, it seemed, were less interesting these days. He knew he had to find a way to leave the past behind, enjoy the present moment with his family, and figure out some plan for the future, but he didn't know where to begin.

He'd never imagined that the hardest part of the presidency would be leaving it behind.

Chapter Seven

Balmoral Castle, Scotland
June 1969

s the car pulled into the enormous driveway, the youngest member of the family couldn't contain her excitement. "Mommy, it's a real castle!"

She smiled at her daughter. "Yes it is, baby. And you're about to meet a real-life Queen."

Aurora was stunned into uncharacteristic silence by this news. With Caroline and John immersed in their own conversation, she took advantage of the brief pause and turned to her husband. "Are you looking forward to the weekend?"

He nodded. "Though I still can't really believe we're here. Not the typical family vacation you were planning, huh?"

She smiled and shook her head. "I suppose not. But when the Queen invites you for a visit to her castle in the countryside, I don't think there's any way of saying no."

The invitation had arrived a few weeks ago and had been a complete surprise to him, although not as surprising as what he'd learned when he'd asked Jackie about it.

They were relaxing over drinks one evening after the kids had gone to bed. There were only two weeks left until they departed for London, the first stop on their European summer trip, and she was listing off the places they should visit in the city when she casually dropped a bombshell into the itinerary discussion.

"Oh, and I just found out we'll need to add on a few days in Scotland."

"Sounds fine. Where exactly?"

"Balmoral Castle." She looked up from her notepad and took a sip of wine, assessing his reaction.

"You mean—the royal castle? Queen Elizabeth's summer home?"

"That's right. She invited the whole family for a visit."

He stared at her, trying to make some sense out of her words. "Queen Elizabeth invited us to her summer house in Scotland?"

"That's right. The kids too."

"That makes absolutely no sense."

"It doesn't? Why not?"

He didn't know where to begin. "Well, first of all, we haven't seen her in almost a decade. And, well, she's the Queen of England. Does she make a habit of inviting strangers to visit her at her castle?" He assumed the answer was no, at least not strangers who no longer held any formal office in their countries.

"We're not strangers. Like you said, we've met them before."

"That's right, and as I recall, the two of you didn't particularly hit it off."

She shook her head. "That's not true. It just took us a little while to get to know each other."

"And when did you do that exactly?" He was still puzzled; none of this made any sense.

"Oh, we've been writing to each other for years." She glanced back down at her notebook nonchalantly, and he couldn't help thinking she was rather enjoying the shocked expression on his face.

"You and Queen Elizabeth have been writing to each other? You're kidding."

"I'm certainly not. We write each other—oh, every few months, I guess."

"But why? And since when? How did this even start?"

She smiled at his surprise, but then her face became serious. "Well, she wrote to me after . . . after you were shot." Her voice dropped, and she looked down into her wineglass.

"She did?" He was startled.

"Yes, she sent me a very kind letter. I wrote back, and then she wrote back, and, well, after that we just kind of kept it going."

"So what you're telling me is, you're pen pals with the Queen of England." He shook his head in amazement. "Only you, Jackie."

She smiled. "Anyway, in my last letter I mentioned we'd be visiting England, and when she heard that. she invited us to Balmoral for a weekend. Three days of horses and corgis. Are you on board?"

He laughed, shaking his head. "I'm not going to turn down an invitation like that. Especially when the two of you have such a long-standing correspondence going. Tell her we'll be honored to come."

They walked down the long, darkly furnished hallway together. As befitted a summer home, this place was more laid-back than Buckingham Palace, but it was clearly still a royal residence. She had a million questions about its art and décor and the history behind it all, but she decided to save them for later. It felt appropriate to let her hostess make the first conversational move.

"I'm so delighted you were able to come," Queen Elizabeth said, turning to her with a slightly shy smile. She smiled back, feeling in the Queen's expression an echo of herself. Two shy, introverted women who, through circumstances largely beyond their control, had been thrust into very public lives on the front lines of history.

"Of course. It was so kind of you to invite us. My children are so excited." She smiled again, remembering their meeting with the royal children earlier today. "Aurora especially. She was so thrilled to meet Princess Anne! I don't think her friends back home will ever stop hearing about how she met a real princess this summer." She laughed. "It was very sweet of her to offer to take the children around and show them the castle grounds."

They had entered a spacious room with comfortable chairs, and Elizabeth (as she would have to get used to calling her, at least in her own mind) gestured graciously for her to have a seat. "I'm sure they'll all have a lovely time together. And Prince Phillip and President Kennedy should be having a nice chat over drinks and cigars right now, I should imagine."

She nodded, smiling slightly. "I'm sure."

"I thought it would be nice for us to have a chance to chat privately," Elizabeth said. "I've so many questions I want to ask you."

She was surprised, and it must have shown on her face, for the Queen laughed.

"Of course. Ask away, Your Majesty." *Am I still supposed to call her that? What are the rules of protocol, once a Queen—of a country that once ruled your own, no less— becomes a friend?*

The Queen poured tea for them both and settled back to sip her drink. "So how are you enjoying life after the White House, Mrs. Kennedy?"

She paused, sipping her tea while giving the question real consideration. "To be honest, I'm enjoying it immensely."

The Queen nodded. "I rather thought you might."

She smiled wryly, glancing down into her cup. "It just feels so . . . freeing I suppose. No schedules or protocol to follow, no rules; we just get to be a normal family. Even this trip: I've been planning it ever since we packed up and moved to our new house in Virginia."

"And what is your house like?"

"It's perfect. Right in the middle of Virginia horse country. Lots of space, plenty of privacy. I ride every day, I read books, swim; the children love it too. It's all I could ask for."

She heard herself utter the words, and somehow, hearing herself say them aloud made her realize for the first time that they didn't sound quite right.

All *she* could ask for, yes. That was certainly true. But she wasn't the only person whose happiness or lack thereof in the new house needed to be considered.

Queen Elizabeth regarded her guest in silence, waiting for her to say more. After a moment, she continued. "But as to how my husband is enjoying it—that's another question."

"He isn't enjoying the house?"

She shook her head. "That's not it, exactly. It's more that he isn't enjoying much of anything these days."

It was the first time she'd spoken these words to anyone or even acknowledged this truth to herself. She and the children were thriving in their post-White House life. Her husband, on the other hand, had rarely seemed less happy.

She hadn't intended to speak these thoughts aloud, but suddenly they were tumbling out of her, as if she'd just been waiting for the right confidante to share them with.

"The truth is, ever since we left the White House, Jack has seemed . . . restless? Directionless? Like he doesn't know what to do next, how to occupy himself. I love the privacy, the freedom of our lives now, but he doesn't see the appeal of any of it. And he just seems so . . ." She paused, grasping for the right word.

"Unhappy?" Elizabeth suggested in a soft voice.

She shook her head. "Lost." *And that might be even worse.*

Since the day she'd met him, her husband had been the most dynamic, driven, ambitious man she'd ever known. He'd always known exactly what he wanted, and he'd gone out and against overwhelming odds made it happen. But now, what came next? She didn't know, and clearly neither did he. Watching him amble through his days with no direction or purpose was a completely foreign experience for her, and not one she enjoyed. She'd been so full of hope that his retirement would allow them to finally live a normal family life. That had been her dream. But what if his only real dream had already been achieved and relegated to the history books? What if he would never again find anything to make him as happy as being President had done? What if everything in his life simply went downhill from here—at least in his own mind?

What if I'm not enough for him?

She sighed, feeling unsettled and embarrassed; this certainly wasn't how she'd imagined her first in-person conversation with the Queen in nearly a decade would unfold. But so much had changed since their last meeting in 1962, for better and for worse.

"May I ask you a very personal question, Your Majesty?" The words were formal, but her tone was softer, more intimate. The Queen nodded, gazing steadily at her.

"How would you feel if you woke up one morning and you weren't Queen anymore? If you had to find something else, something completely different, to do with your life?"

Queen Elizabeth paused for a moment, looking down into her teacup. When she lifted her eyes, she responded slowly, as if considering every word carefully.

"I've known I would be Queen since I was ten years old, ever since the day my uncle abdicated." She glanced down again; this was clearly a painful subject she would have preferred not to address. "It was never a matter of if, only when, I'd assume the throne. It's always been my destiny, what my entire life has been about and always will be. I shall be the monarch of Great Britain until the day I die." Her tone was calm, matter of fact, but there was a trace of resignation in it as well.

"For your husband, it's a very different situation. He chose to pursue the presidency; it was never guaranteed that he would achieve it. And now he's had to give it up, perhaps just when he felt he was getting good at it. I know it took me at least a decade to feel I'd really found my footing as Queen. But please, don't repeat that to anyone."

Elizabeth smiled slightly, and she returned the smile a bit hesitantly.

"What I mean to say is, our situations are completely different. But I can certainly imagine how difficult a time this might be for him. Even if, to be quite honest, a part of me does envy the freedom that the two of you and your children have now. But I know if, as you say, I ever had to stop being Queen, it would be very difficult to stop thinking of myself as such. To adjust to a life where I wasn't serving my country, my people, in that way."

She nodded. "That makes sense."

"But, as you know, people are resilient. I'm sure he'll adapt in time. But it may take him a while to discover what his next steps, his second act, should look like. I'm sure his first act will be a difficult one to follow." Queen Elizabeth smiled.

She nodded. "Yes. I just wish there were some way I could help him figure it all out. I hate seeing him unhappy."

Elizabeth nodded sympathetically. "I have no doubt you will, in time. And that he'll figure out what to do next with his life. I know I'll be very curious to see what he decides on."

"That makes two of us, then." They both laughed, and she began to feel a bit better. She was also filled with a new resolve. As soon as they returned home from their European sojourn, she would have this conversation with her husband.

"Thank you for listening," she said, feeling a bit embarrassed but also lighter than she had in months. "How can I repay you?"

The Queen smiled. "You can call me by my first name, if I may do the same. And you can invite me to visit your horse farm in Virginia. I think I'm due for a trip back to the States."

They both laughed, "Absolutely."

And at long last, the conversation turned from husbands to horses.

———————

The rest of their summer vacation passed all too quickly. After London and the weekend at Balmoral they visited Paris, the Cote d'Azur, then Italy and Greece. Touring the ancient monuments, swimming in the waters off Capri, and sailing around the Greek islands in their sailboat, doing their best to avoid photographers and reporters at every stop, the five of them finally had the glorious, relatively private summer vacation she had dreamed of for so long. It was perfect.

Jack seemed to perk up during their travels, especially while they sailed around the Aegean for the final week of the trip. All too soon, however, it was time to head back to the US. And while she was sad their summer sojourn was over, she was also glad to return to Virginia and their family's new home.

On July 20, the five of them sat in their living room in front of the television, watching as one of her husband's most audacious dreams became a reality: an American astronaut walked on the moon. As they listened to Neil Armstrong declare "That's one small step for man, one giant leap for mankind," they sat in stunned silence like millions of viewers around the world, taking in this seemingly impossible sight that Jack's vision and determination had made possible.

"I'm so proud of you, Jack," she murmured to him that evening as they were getting ready for bed. "What an incredible thing you've done."

He smiled slightly. "Well, I'm not actually the one who set foot on the moon, but thanks."

"You know what I mean. You had the vision, the dream. You made this happen. This is something people will remember forever, that children will study in history books for generations, and it happened because of you."

He looked pleased, but soon his smile faded. She decided that now was as good a time as any for the talk she knew they needed to have at long last.

"Queen Elizabeth said something interesting to me while we were at Balmoral," she began, sitting on her side of the bed and concentrating on rubbing lotion onto her hands. "She said that she's very curious to know what your second act is going to look like."

"Did she?" he asked, leaning back against the pillows with a sigh. Even in the flush of this historic moment, perhaps even because of it, he looked drawn, resigned. She knew she had to break through this defensive posture.

"I told her she wasn't the only one." She turned to look over her shoulder at Jack and found him staring at the ceiling as though fascinated by the swirling patterns above the bed. After a moment, with her eyes steadily fixed on him, he turned toward her.

"Well, tell her I'm still figuring it out."

"Are you, Jack? Because I don't see much sign of it from here."

He sat up, looking directly at her for the first time. "What does that mean?"

She sighed, shaking her head, wondering how to proceed without making him feel like she was criticizing him.

"I just mean that, ever since we left the White House, you've seemed sort of adrift."

He was silent for a moment, then finally he nodded. "You're right. That's exactly it. I'm adrift." He didn't say anything else for a moment, and she waited for him to continue.

"Funny word, isn't it? Like a leaf floating in a stream. No purpose, no direction, just floating along."

"Is that how you feel? How you've felt these past few months?"

"Yes." He sighed, but it seemed no other insights were forthcoming.

She took a deep breath, steeling herself for the conversation ahead. "Jack, listen to me. I know this must be a difficult transition for you . . ."

"It's not a transition." He spoke more forcefully. "That's not how it feels. *Transition* implies moving from one thing to another, and that's not the way this feels at all. It just feels like . . ." He paused, as if he were saying more than he'd meant to, and looked down.

"Jack?" She stared at him, willing him to look back up at her.

He did, and after a moment he sighed deeply. "It feels like the end."

His words hit her hard, and she responded forcefully. "Jack, that's ridiculous. Just because you're not president any more doesn't mean your life is over."

He looked into her eyes, and she suddenly felt a terrible, stabbing fear. Was that really how he felt? Did he feel his life was over because his presidency was?

"It doesn't," she repeated, more fiercely than she'd intended to. Because she had to make him believe it.

He started to speak, but she rolled on before he could say any more, the words finally pouring out after months of keeping them inside, hoping fruitlessly that things would somehow get better. But sitting back and waiting hadn't yielded any results, and this was too important to ignore any longer.

"Jack, listen to me. I want you to be happy. I want all of us to be happy, but this malaise of yours can't go on any longer. We can't go on like this. I know leaving the White House was hard. I know figuring out your next steps must feel overwhelming, but you have to start trying. Pacing around the garden all day, sitting watching TV for hours, ignoring your friends—that's not you, Jack. I've known you for nearly two decades, and I've never seen you like this before. And I hate it. I hate seeing you so unhappy, so unfulfilled. And it doesn't have to be this way. Because your life isn't over, not even close. You're only fifty-two. You have decades left ahead of you, and you need to find something to do with them that will make you happy, give you some sense of purpose again. Because this isn't—"

She broke off abruptly, shook her head, and said more quietly, "This isn't what you survived Dallas for, Jack. You weren't born to be President for eight years and then spend the rest of your life pining away for the past, living this gloomy shadow existence. You're better than that. You're stronger and more resilient, and I know you can figure out what to do with the rest of your life and find meaning in it. You have to try. For me, for the children, and for yourself."

He stared back at her for a moment as the force of her outburst washed over him, and then, suddenly, his face seemed to crumple. "I'm sorry, Jackie."

"For what?"

He shook his head. "You're right, Jackie, I know you are. And I'm sorry I've been the way I've been these past few months. Especially since you've been completely the opposite. I see every day how happy you are here. How much you love our life now. And I wish I felt the same way. But the honest-to-God truth is, I just feel useless. I'm barely fifty, and it feels like the most important part of my life is over, and I don't know what to do about it."

He continued in a rush, as though now that he'd finally begun speaking about this he couldn't get the words out fast enough.

"You know, it's like my whole life I've been climbing up a ladder. I finished college; I went off to fight in the war. My brother died, and suddenly all the family's expectations, hopes, were put on me. So I ran for Congress at twenty-nine, and I won; then I ran for Senate, and I won. Then I ran for president, and I won. And suddenly, I realized there was nowhere left to climb. I'd made it to the top, become President of the United States, against all the odds. And I loved it, even the hard parts. Looking back, Jackie, I loved every single minute of it. And now I can't get it back. I can never be President again, and I don't know what to do with the rest of my life."

She was silent for a full minute, her husband's words swirling in her mind. He was looking at her as though now that the words were finally out and he'd put this truth before her, he was desperately hoping she could help him make sense of it. At last she spoke.

"You know, Jack—I think you may be looking at all this the wrong way."

"What do you mean?"

"What you said a minute ago about climbing the ladder? How that's what you've been doing your whole life? It's true, and yes, that's one way to look at life, but it's not the only way."

"What's the other way?"

"Well, instead of imagining yourself climbing a ladder, maybe you can think of this next step in your life as setting down roots, sinking deeper into the earth. Find a place to belong and plant yourself there, and watch yourself grow year by year."

He shook his head. "It's a nice metaphor, but I don't know what it means. Not in terms of my life."

"My point is, you've spent your whole life climbing a ladder upward, fixated on a single goal. And now you've achieved it. But instead of seeing that as an ending, maybe it can be a new beginning. Now is your chance to do something new, something different, explore a new part of yourself. Isn't there something else you've always wanted to try that you could now that you have this chance?"

He shook his head. He couldn't think of anything.

After a pause she said, "Remember when we were first married, the year you had your surgery and spent all those months recovering? You couldn't be a politician, so you found something new to focus on instead. You became a writer."

He smiled slightly, shaking his head again. "I wrote one book—well, two, counting my college thesis. I hardly think that makes me a writer."

"Of course it does. And in case you've forgotten, that one book won the Pulitzer Prize. It was excellent, Jack.

Profiles in Courage made people think about history in an entirely new way. That's a real accomplishment, and you shouldn't take it lightly."

He was silent, mulling this over. "Well, maybe you're right. I guess I should get started on my memoirs."

"Of course you should, when you're ready, but why stop there? Why not do more? You love writing, Jack. I saw how much you loved it when we worked on the book together. And you love history too; it's part of what has shaped you, made you the man you are. So why not take this opportunity to write a book about history, some part of it that fascinates you, and share your passion with the world? If you're looking for a new purpose in your life, what greater one could there possibly be?"

He paused, considering her words. For the first time in months, she saw an expression on his face that had been absent for so long: the look he got when he was genuinely excited about something, when an idea took hold of him and began to come to fruition. And then, he looked up at her and smiled.

"You know, Jackie, I think you may have something there."

"Really?"

"Yes. I never really thought of myself as a writer or imagined that's what I'd do in my retirement, but maybe it's worth a shot?"

She nodded emphatically, overjoyed at finally seeing the spark of excitement in his eyes about trying something new. His second act. "Absolutely. I think this could be perfect for you."

"I just have one thing to ask you."

"What is it?"

"Will you help me?"

"Help you? What do you mean?"

"I mean, will you help me write a book? Like you did last time? I couldn't have written *Profiles in Courage* without you, Jackie."

She smiled, looking down and blushing slightly. "Yes. I remember the book dedication."

"It was all true. You helped create that book: researching, editing, just sharing your thoughts with me during the whole process. I couldn't have done it without you. And if I'm going to try writing another book, I only want to do it if I can work with you. If we can create something together."

She looked pleased, but also a bit skeptical. "But Jack, I mean——sure, I helped you before. And I loved it. But I'm not a professional editor or researcher. You could easily find someone more experienced than I am to do all of that."

"I don't want anyone else. I want you. I want us to do this together. There's no one in the world I trust more than you, Jackie. And if I'm really going to start writing again, I want you by my side every step of the way."

He smiled at her, and all her uncertainty faded away as his words washed over her. *I don't want anyone else. I want you.* How many years she'd waited to hear him say that to her, and now, regardless of the context, she knew there was no way she could refuse him. She felt suddenly flush with excitement for everything that lay ahead: a new chapter for the two of them.

"So, will you do it? Will you write a book with me?"

She smiled radiantly, reaching over to brush the hair back from his forehead. "Of course I will, Jack."

"Good. So, shall we get started tomorrow morning?"

She laughed, delighted by how his mood had changed so quickly after the gloomy past few months since he'd left the White House behind. "That sounds perfect. And next time I write to Elizabeth—"

"Elizabeth?"

"Queen Elizabeth. We're officially on a first-name basis now."

"Of course you are. Go on."

"I'll be very happy to tell her you're about to begin your second act."

He shook his head. "We're about to begin it, you mean. Together."

"Yes, that's right. Together."

She smiled, wrapped her arms around his neck, and they fell back against the pillows, entwined as one.

Chapter Eight

Papeete, Tahiti
September 1973

The breeze blew gently across the sandbar, so bright white that it stood out against the turquoise waters as if it had been painted there, a dash of white in an ocean of blue. It looked unreal, as if no place in the world had the right to be as stunningly beautiful as this tiny sliver in the Pacific at what seemed like the end of the earth. It felt like a place designed to hold only two people who had traveled halfway around the world to seek it out for a magical escape.

She stood transfixed, her sarong blowing lightly in the wind as she watched the sun begin to dip in the sky for what she knew would be another spectacular sunset, just like the one they'd seen the night before hours after they'd first arrived in this paradise. As her eyes remained glued to the horizon, she felt his arms wrap around her from behind and heard him murmur, "Happy anniversary."

She half turned in his arms, smiling. "Happy second honeymoon."

And they fell silent together, staring out at the ocean and the setting sun and trying to absorb the beauty of this moment before it faded into memory forever.

It had been more than four years since this new chapter of their lives had begun the morning after their talk on the night of the moon landing. As they'd decided that evening, more on a whim than anything else, they had begun their first post-White House adventure together, writing books.

The first one, a biography of several of the more obscure Founding Fathers, was published in 1971. It was released to great fanfare, sold out in days, and quickly required a second printing and then a third to keep up with the demand by the public for the ex-president's writing.

The book was not just a popular success but a critical one as well. Historians praised its precise details and accuracy, while reviewers rhapsodized over the writing itself, the way it fulfilled the cliché goal of making history come alive even for those who'd never had much knowledge of or interest it before.

But the book's success wasn't its author's alone. From the day he began writing, Jackie sat by his side in a spare bedroom they transformed into an office or at the dining room table late into the evenings, helping to shape the story page by page. ("Mom and Dad have more homework than we do," Caroline commented to her brother and sister one evening as they watched their parents type and scribble away for hours after dinner.) She researched and double-checked facts and dates, drawing on her own love of history to dig enthusiastically into the topic at hand. And she also served as the book's principal editor, streamlining and polishing the text to keep the narrative tightly focused while retaining all the lush historical details that made the story so fascinating to millions of readers.

When the book was released, the title page acknowledged her contribution with these words: "Edited by Mrs. Jacqueline Kennedy."

She had tried to protest that this was unnecessary ("No one cares who edits a book, only who writes it")," but her husband insisted. "There's no way we're publishing this without giving you the credit you deserve."

The publication of the book and its status as a joint project between the former President and the First Lady quickly brought Jack and Jackie back into the public eye. They declined to be interviewed about the book, but its spectacular success had returned them to the spotlight regardless, as did a series of other events.

In September 1971, the John F. Kennedy Center for the Performing Arts opened, a symbol of the former president's legacy as a promoter of culture during his time in office. Jack and Jackie attended the debut performance, where he officially opened the new center and gave a brief speech to acknowledge the moment and declare his enthusiasm for the arts. Jackie had written his remarks without being asked.

"Here," she said, handing him a few typewritten pages the day before the event. "These should do nicely."

"Thanks," he said, scanning her words and nodding his approval. When he delivered his speech the next evening, he followed them to the letter until he reached the end. He finished by offering an extemporaneous addition praising his wife's role as a cultural ambassador during her eight years as First Lady and noting that the Kennedy Center would never have been created without her dedicated vision.

She stood by her husband's side, radiant in a dark blue floor-length Cassini gown, and smiled in surprised delight at his final words.

"That really wasn't necessary, Jack," she murmured as he took her hand, and they walked together towards the presidential box, which would be theirs for the night, as President Nixon had declined to attend—perhaps all too aware of the contrast that would be struck between him and his predecessor if he did.

"Of course it was," he replied. "I mean, let's be honest; you're the patron of the arts in our family. I was just along for the ride for eight years."

She laughed, shaking her head. The building full of photographers dutifully took note of this intimate exchange between husband and wife, even though no one could hear their words. The next day the photographs were on the front page of every newspaper in America.

"You look beautiful," he observed as they looked at the pictures in the paper the next morning.

"Thank you," she smiled. "I told you that gown Oleg made would be well worth it, didn't I?"

He laughed. "It's paid for itself already." He shook his head, feeling glad that with age he'd acquired enough wisdom to stop monitoring (or complaining about) how much she spent on clothes, household furnishings, and just about anything else. Life was short, as he'd been reminded after Dallas, and fights over clothing budgets were ultimately far more trouble than they were worth. And it was true; she had looked absolutely radiant last night in her new dress. And at this point in their lives, seeing his wife happy was the thing he'd come to value above everything else.

Within a few weeks, copies of Jackie's dress were being churned out and were flying off the shelves of boutiques faster than they could be stocked. Even out of the White House, removed from public life and doing their best to avoid unnecessary attention, the glow had not yet worn off the Kennedys. America, it appeared, still loved Jack and Jackie.

In 1972, Bobby decided the time was right to make his presidential run.

The country had had three years of Richard Nixon's presidency. While he had presided over a relatively calm period following the madness of the late 1960s, he had failed utterly to captivate the nation the way his predecessor had. He was, it appeared, a placeholder, and a somewhat suspicious, untrustworthy one at that. It seemed entirely possible that he could be defeated by the right opponent who could seize the moment and make a case for change.

On a cold winter day in February 1972, Senator Kennedy threw his hat into the ring for the Democratic Party's presidential nomination in front of a packed crowd in his adopted state of New York. Standing behind him, bundled up against the chilly wind, stood all the members of the Kennedy family, with Jack and Jackie at the center, smiling and waving to the crowd after his speech finished to wild applause.

"I really think Bobby's going to do it," he told Jackie later that evening as they sank onto the sofa in the suite of their hotel room.

"Did you ever doubt it?"

"Not him, just the timing. I thought maybe it was too soon, just four years after we left the White House. But that crowd today, his speech—I've just got a feeling. He's going to go all the way." He smiled, feeling both proud and, he had to admit to himself, a bit wistful about the possibility of his brother taking up the job he'd left so recently. He had moved on, and both he and Jackie were happy with their new life; but it still felt strange to imagine Bobby and Ethel living in the house he and Jackie had occupied so recently. It was as if they were already ghosts, relics of American history, though still very much alive.

"Which means we have something to talk about."

She looked at him in surprise. "What's that?"

"The campaign." He looked at her and saw the awareness dawn in her eyes.

"He's going to want you to campaign with him." She nodded. "And you're going to want to help him."

"Of course I am. But it's not just about what I want."

She gazed at him steadily, without speaking. Then finally, she said, "I want you to do what makes you happy, Jack. Whatever you think is right."

He couldn't hide his surprise. "Four years ago, you felt differently, as I remember."

She nodded. "Yes, I certainly did."

"So what's changed?"

She paused, then shook her head. "It just feels different somehow. The world feels a bit less scary than it did back then. And this isn't just another Democrat you'd be supporting out of a sense of duty. It's Bobby. How can you not help him become president? How can *we* not, if we have the chance?"

"I agree. But if you have any doubts . . ."

She sighed. "I can't say I don't have any worries, Jack. I'm always going to worry about you, about your safety. But we can't live our lives in fear either. This is important, and I don't think it would feel right if we didn't help Bobby win this election."

He smiled. "You never cease to amaze me."

She laughed in surprise. "That's good, I suppose, but why?"

He said, his voice more serious, "Because even when you have every reason to want to avoid something, if you think it's right, you always decide to do it. You're the bravest person I know."

She smiled, unable to hide her pleasure at his words. "Anyway. I think you should campaign with Bobby on one condition."

"What's that?"

"I'm coming with you. You can only campaign if I'm by your side. At least that way I can keep an eye on you." *And keep you safe.*

He grinned. "Deal."

On November 8, 1972, it became official: the Kennedys were heading back to the White House. Bobby ran up an impressive margin of victory against Richard Nixon, consigning him to be a one-term president and marking the beginning of a new era in American political history.

As much pride and delight as she felt for her brother-in-law's success, if she were honest with herself, her main feeling on election night 1972 was one of profound relief. No more campaign rallies and public speeches and events for her and Jack. While she'd meant what she'd said about supporting Bobby, the ghosts of Dallas had never completely vanished from her mind. Often, during events packed with friendly and even euphoric crowds, she found herself plastering a smile on her face while her eyes darted around the room or the plaza, searching for anyone out of the ordinary, a twin of the man with a rifle whose actions a decade earlier had so nearly altered the course of her life forever.

But this time, all was calm. Perhaps the country was beginning to come to its senses again, she thought. In any case, once Bobby was sworn in on January 20, 1973, with her and Jack looking on proudly as he took the oath of office, followed by another dizzying round of inaugural balls that evening, she felt more than ready to leave the campaign trail behind and return to civilian life again.

She and Jack quickly began working on a new book, this one about Thomas Jefferson and Alexander Hamilton's complex relationship, and as they plunged into the writing and research process, life began to return to normal. One evening in August, after spending hours writing and editing their new project side by side after dinner, they collapsed onto the sofa with a bottle of wine, finally ready to relax at the end of a long but satisfying day, when Jack brought up something she'd completely forgotten.

"You know—our anniversary is only a few weeks away."

"You're kidding! It can't be. Isn't this still July?"

"No, that was last month, don't you remember? We celebrated your birthday at Hyannis Port."

"Oh, that's right," she nodded in recollection. Her forty-fourth birthday hadn't been a major milestone, but they'd still had a small family gathering to mark the occasion. She couldn't believe that had been a month ago already as she marveled at how quickly the summer was flying. Her husband seemed to feel much the same way.

"This year's gone awfully fast, hasn't it?" he mused, sounding a bit wistful. "I feel like it's all moving so quickly. Soon we'll be ready for the retirement home."

She laughed. "I don't think we're there quite yet, Jack. We've got a few more good years left in us."

"Well, let's enjoy them then. I was thinking: this is our twentieth wedding anniversary. That's a pretty big deal, wouldn't you say? Seems like it deserves a celebration."

She smiled, nodding. "What did you have in mind?'

"Well, why don't we take a trip? Just the two of us?"

"I'd love that. Where should we go?"

"Anywhere in the world. Wherever you'd like."

She smiled in delight. "Well now, that requires some thought." She stood up and walked over to the bookshelf, pulling down the bulky atlas from the wall and then settling back on the couch and flipping through it.

"Hmm . . . we could go to Europe again, but we've been so many places there already. I'd love to visit somewhere new. Somewhere tropical, maybe, and isolated. Where no one can find us." She frowned slightly, remembering their vacation to Greece a few years ago, which had been delightful but marred by intrusive paparazzi at every stop. Not this time. If the two of them were going to take a trip to celebrate their wedding anniversary, she was determined to go someplace where they'd be able to enjoy total privacy.

She paged through the atlas until she reached the back and paused over an image of the islands of the South Pacific. One place name, suffused with romance, popped out at her immediately: *Tahiti.*

"How about an island? I've always wanted to visit Tahiti. It sounds magical, don't you think?"

He nodded, looking over her shoulder at the tiny dot in the middle of the vast blue ocean. "Well, the last time I was in the South Pacific, my boat was sunk. But I'm guessing that won't happen this time."

She laughed. "This trip will be less dramatic for you, I promise. But really, I've always wanted to go to Tahiti ever since I read a story about it when I was little."

"Well, that settles it then. Tahiti it is."

"And it's part of French Polynesia, so at least we speak the language."

"You mean, you speak it. But I trust you to navigate us around."

She smiled, closed the book, and said, "All right, then. Time to start planning."

Within a week she'd arranged everything. She'd booked their private accommodation on an island that was little more than a sandbar, with the necessary residual Secret Service protection ensconced a short distance away on the shore, just in case. She'd scheduled their flight on a private plane from California to the capital city Papeete with no fanfare in order to keep the lowest profile possible. And she'd arranged for her mother to stay with the children for a week at their house; school had just begun for the year, and it would have been too disruptive now to send them away. All the pieces were in place for a week of relaxation in the middle of a tropical paradise.

"Our second honeymoon," she declared, as they stepped on board the plane to begin their journey to Papeete on a warm September day.

"Our second honeymoon," he agreed, smiling.

———————————

It was rather odd, she reflected, that it had taken them twenty years to plan an anniversary trip. But somehow the timing had never been right. On their fifth anniversary, Caroline had been only a few months old, and Jack had been running for reelection to the Senate with one eye already firmly fixed on Pennsylvania Avenue. Their tenth anniversary, in 1963, had been a quiet and solemn one, coming only a month after baby Patrick's death. And in 1968, their fifteenth anniversary had coincided with the presidential election and Jack's final few months as president, which had hardly seemed like an ideal time to take an extended romantic vacation. But now, as they prepared to mark two decades of marriage, it seemed the perfect moment had finally arrived.

Tahiti was every bit as beautiful as she had dreamed, and from the moment she stepped off the plane into the tropical sunshine, she could feel herself begin to relax. When they arrived at their private bungalow, situated on a stretch of white sandy beach lapped by turquoise waters, she was instantly mesmerized by the island's beauty, yet felt they could spend the next week in their enormous bedroom with its magnificent view of the sea and be perfectly happy.

"So, what do you think?" her husband asked as they strolled across the sand towards the setting sun. "Better than Acapulco?"

She smiled, remembering their rapturous first honeymoon in Mexico. How young they'd been then, she mused; how completely unaware of everything the world had in store for the two of them, both good and bad.

"Well, I don't know yet. But so far, I'd say our second honeymoon is off to a pretty wonderful start."

"And it hasn't even really begun yet." They sat down together on the sand, and she was taking in the dramatic sky with its pre-sunset pinks and purples and golds, when she suddenly caught a glimpse of an object out of the corner of her eye. "Is that a radio?"

"Why, yes, it is. I figured we could kick off our first night here with a little dancing."

She stared at him in surprise, then burst out laughing. "Really? That's so unlike you, Jack."

"How do you mean?"

"Well—you've never been that much of a romantic, at least not in the traditional sense."

"Oh, come on. That's not fair."

"You sent me a single telegram during our entire courtship."

He shook his head. "I'm pretty sure that's not true. I think it got printed in that biography about you last year, and now you think it's what really happened. But I'm sure I wrote to you more than once while we were dating."

"I remember my own life, Jack."

He grinned, looking a bit sheepish. "Okay, fair enough. Is it too late to say I'm sorry?"

She smiled. "I think you can just get it in under the wire."

"Good. And now, let me prove to you that I can, in fact, be romantic."

"At least once every two decades."

He laughed, flicking through the radio channels.

"You'll never get any reception, Jack. We're in the middle of nowhere."

"I think I'm picking up something—ah! Here we go."

They both fell silent, straining to hear as he turned up the volume. A moment later, the lyrics to *Monster Mash* began to come through.

"Hmm . . . not quite what I had in mind."

"I agree. Can we get any other stations?"

"I'm guessing Tahitian radio doesn't have too many options, but let's see . . ." He flipped through the machine's dial, and a moment later they heard the opening lines of *Space Oddity*.

"Well, that clearly won't work either."

She sighed. "It's fine, Jack. We don't need any music. Just come and sit down and watch the sunset with me."

"No, let me give it another try; I'm sure we can find something better."

"Well, it can't get much worse." She laughed, eyeing her husband as he fiddled with the radio.

"Wait! I think this could be it. What do you think?"

It took a moment for the tinny radio signal to come clear, but then she heard, faintly, the opening chords to *My Love*.

"Paul McCartney? I thought you'd gone off him after the Beatles broke up."

"Well, I did prefer him in the Beatles. But times change. Nothing lasts forever, right?"

She almost pointed out that the entire purpose of this trip was to celebrate the fact that some things did in fact last, despite all the odds. But then she looked into his eyes, and he was smiling at her and holding out his hand, and she decided not to get hung up on details.

"It's perfect." She took his hand, and he pulled her up and into his arms. She rested her head on his shoulder as he swirled her around on the sand, a bit more slowly than he had at their wedding twenty years ago, but the feeling of being wrapped in his embrace was still the same.

Some things did last, she thought. Not forever, maybe. But twenty years, right now, felt more than good enough.

The next few days slipped by like a dream. The days ticked past languidly yet all too quickly as they swam and water-skied in brilliant blue waters, lounged on the beach reading novels while drinking tropical concoctions, and dined on their private sandbar every evening before retiring to their bungalow for the night. Before she knew it, their time in Tahiti was half over. She wished she could slow it down, but somehow the days marched on relentlessly despite her secret desire to stay here alone with her husband in this magical island paradise forever.

And then in the middle of their blissful vacation, something unexpected happened. For the first time in years, her nightmares returned.

They were lying in their enormous bed one evening, lulled to sleep by exhaustion from the day's and night's activities and the gentle ocean breeze, when she suddenly woke with a jolt. She experienced a moment of blind panic that felt all too familiar as she struggled to ground herself, but part of her mind remained back in a hellscape she thought she'd long since left behind.

She reached out her hand and felt Jack before she saw him, as her eyes slowly adjusted to the dim moonlight. He was there, of course, sleeping peacefully beside her, his own dreams apparently untroubled. She pulled her knees up and buried her head against them, trying to shake free of the visions to remind herself where she was. *You're in Tahiti, on your second honeymoon. Jack is right next to you. He's fine. You're fine. Everything is fine.*

After a few minutes of repeating these words to herself, she felt a bit calmer, but suddenly restless. She had an overwhelming urge to leave the room, to walk outside until the dark clouds in her head had time to dissipate before they could find their way into this perfect idyll and contaminate it with worry and fear. She glanced over and saw that her husband was still fast asleep, and she carefully slipped on a light robe and crept out of the room, taking pains not to wake him. She didn't want him to know where she was going—or why.

The specific dream vision that had jolted her awake tonight was the one secret she had kept from Jack over the past ten years. As she paced down the beach alone, staring out at the gently rolling ocean, she remembered the conversation they'd had on another beach five years ago when she'd asked him not to campaign for Hubert Humphrey. She recalled how terrified she'd been that day of what might await him in the cesspool of America in 1968, back when the entire country felt as if it had burst into flame, and how relieved she'd been when he'd promised not to venture out onto the campaign trail that fall.

And she remembered his words that day, how his voice had dropped and his tone had turned gentle as he'd told her, *If you're upset or worried or afraid, I want you to tell me.* And she'd known that he meant it. And from that day onward, she had.

It had been an enormous relief once she realized that she really could share her darkest fears with Jack, that she didn't constantly need to put up a façade of being happy or brave or stoic when in reality, the world they were living in had left her all too frequently wracked with fear. Dallas and its aftermath had left their mark on her, as she knew they must have on him as well. But they hadn't talked about it much at the time, and as the years had passed so much else had happened. They'd had Aurora, he'd won reelection and begun his second term, they'd watched their children grow and thrive during the next four years in the White House. She hadn't wanted to sully those glorious, mostly happy days with any discussion of her private fears.

So she'd kept quiet, even when the nightmares woke her up at night, even when her dreams were haunted by the memory of her husband falling over into her lap and losing consciousness as they raced to the hospital. Every second of that ride had felt like an eternity as she prayed they would arrive in time, that he would be okay, that this wouldn't be the end of their story.

As the years passed, however, those memories had begun to lose some of their power over her, and the nightmares that used to wake her up regularly became less frequent. Time seemed to be healing her mental wounds, for the most part. And she'd kept her promise to Jack and begun to talk with him about her fears in a way she would never have been willing to do even a few years earlier.

Now, on the rare occasions she woke up from a nightmare that pulled her back to that horrible day, he knew. And there was no need to conceal her fears from him any longer. *It's all right,* he'd tell her, drawing her into his arms and running his hand through her hair. *It's fine. We're fine. Everything is okay.*

But there remained one secret she hadn't told him, one form the nightmares from Dallas took that she hadn't figured out how to share with him.

She sat down cross-legged on the soft pillowy sand, staring out at the ocean for a moment. Then she closed her eyes, and the images appeared before her again, as real as ever.

But what she saw weren't memories of the actual moments she'd lived that horrid day in Dallas, or of the fearful hours in the hospital that had followed before Jack had woken up and the doctors had assured her that her husband would be all right. She'd relived those memories so many times at this point that they felt almost threadbare. They still had the power to frighten her, but they were familiar. They were the past, not the present. She had learned how to cope with them, as dreadful as they were, after years of painful experience.

What she saw when she closed her eyes was different, and it was not something she could explain, even to herself. Not memories, not recollections of painful past moments, but glimpses of something else. Visions of herself doing things she'd never actually done, as if a filmmaker had spliced extra scenes into her life story that didn't belong but somehow felt hauntingly authentic anyway.

In her mind's eye she saw herself walking, staring straight ahead as throngs of onlookers followed her every move yet made no sound. Her vision was obscured—not by the tears that she refused to let fall but by a dark, half-transparent piece of cloth—a veil.

The vision cut away, and she stood at a gravesite, lighting a flame. She knew who the grave belonged to, of course, but she refused to look at the stone, to acknowledge the enormity of the loss.

It's not real, she told herself—or tried to.

For a long time, she'd pushed these painful visions out of her head as best she could, convinced it was simply her mind playing dark tricks on her after all she'd been through that day. And yet somehow they stayed with her. This phantom version of herself—who she'd come to identify, finally, as the other Jackie, the woman she would have been if things had gone even slightly differently on that November day in Texas—haunted her dreams more intensely than her memories of her husband's shooting. She'd begun, finally, to put the latter visions to rest, but sometimes she thought this ghost Jackie might haunt her till the day she died.

She realized that ghost Jackie wasn't the product of a momentary horror that had had a happy ending. It was a vision of herself in another reality—who she would have been if Jack hadn't survived that day. What her life would have looked like if she'd had to say goodbye to him so soon and miss out on these years they'd been able to spend together with their family. How would she have lived through that alternate future? How would she have survived the nightmarish fate she'd barely avoided all those years ago?

She'd tried for so long to push this ghost away. She'd never told Jack about her. She'd never even acknowledged her existence in the privacy of her own mind. The pain she brought with her was simply too great to bear.

But tonight, she suddenly realized, the vision felt different. She'd glimpsed ghost Jackie again in her dream, but something about her was altered now. She didn't look as sad as in her previous incarnations. She glimpsed a bit of light in her eyes, a smile beginning to return after so many years of pain. And she thought perhaps this was a sign that instead of attempting to avoid her ghostly doppelganger, it was time for the two of them to make peace.

She closed her eyes again and bowed her head as if in prayer.

I'm sorry, she thought. *I'm sorry for everything you've suffered, for having to live the life that I escaped. But you've survived, and I think you'll be okay now. So, I'm going to let you go.*

She opened her eyes and looked up, saw the light from the full moon dancing on the water, and felt suddenly an overwhelming sense of peace. She smiled, and for the first time in the last ten years, she felt something inside her unclench, and a profound sense of calm washed over her.

She understood now why this vision had been so hard to get rid of and why she'd never been able to share this particular fear with Jack. She had to reach this point on her own and become strong and wise enough to move forward without help from him or anyone else.

The final ghost of Dallas, banished at last.

She rose to her feet, shook the sand off her robe, and walked away from the water and toward the bungalow without glancing back.

———————

Time seemed to speed up over the next few days, and before she knew it the last evening of their trip had arrived. They decided to celebrate with a picnic on a remote speck of sand they could see from their bungalow with a palm tree squarely at the center—the perfect spot for imagining themselves as castaways, free, at least temporarily, from the prying eyes of the rest of the world.

"I can't believe it's already our last night here," she remarked wistfully as she unpacked their picnic and passed the bread and cheese to him while he poured two glasses of champagne.

"I know," he agreed, sounding as reluctant as she was for the magical week to end. He lifted his glass and said, "Here's to Tahiti. It was an inspired vacation choice."

"To Tahiti," she echoed, smiling, as she sipped her drink in a celebratory toast. "It's everything I thought it would be and more."

"Better than Greece?"

"Absolutely."

"Better than Paris?"

She thought for a moment, then nodded. "Yes. Though Paris will always be special."

"And now, the real question: is it better than Acapulco?"

She laughed. "Do you mean in terms of location or honeymoon?"

"Both. Which is your favorite honeymoon, now that we've officially had two?"

She replied without hesitation. "This one. Tahiti, second honeymoon. Not a doubt in my mind."

He looked surprised by her conviction. "And why's that?"

She paused, reflecting on how to describe what this week had meant to her.

"Well, our first honeymoon was wonderful, of course. But looking back, we were so young. We really had no idea what we were getting into, did we?"

He nodded. "You're right. Maybe that was for the best, looking back on it now."

She smiled slightly. "Yes, maybe it was. But that's not really what I meant. I was thinking more about how when we got married, we didn't really know what that meant, what our marriage was going to *be*. It was just an idea—it wasn't real yet, to either of us. And now . . ."

She paused, and he prompted her. "And now, twenty years in, what do you think?"

She looked into his eyes and reached out to take his hand. "You know, I loved you from the first moment I saw you, Jack. I know that sounds dramatic or romanticized, but looking back I can see it really is true. If I hadn't married you, my life would have been . . . I don't know what it would have been. And I'm glad I never had to find out."

He smiled back at her, squeezing her hand. "So am I."

"And I guess that's the difference between our first honeymoon and this one. All those questions, all those mysteries about what the future would hold, have been answered. We've been through so much, and yet we're still here together. And twenty years later, I love you so much more than I did back then. I honestly do."

"So, no regrets?" He smiled, but there was a serious edge to his question.

"None at all. Even after everything we've been through and how hard it's been sometimes . . ." Her voice trailed off, and she gazed at the ocean before fixing her eyes on his again. "I wouldn't change where we are now for anything in the world. And I'd do it all again, from the very beginning."

He nodded, looking down for a moment and glancing back up again. "I agree. Although in my case there are some things I'd do differently."

He fell silent, and she squeezed his hand. She knew what he was referring to, and knew that he'd never speak those thoughts aloud. But that was okay with her. After their conversation in Dallas he'd never made any reference to the promise he'd made to her that day, but it didn't matter. Dallas had changed him in ways that probably nothing else could have, and it had changed them. They had moved forward from that day side by side, looking toward the future rather than the past, and she felt that was the way it should be. There was nothing to be gained by looking back, not when they still had the rest of their lives ahead of them. They were here together now; they were happy, and nothing else mattered.

"You know," he said, breaking into her reflections, "you're the best thing that ever happened to me in my whole life, Jackie. And I know I don't say it often enough, but it's true. The truth is . . ." He looked out to the ocean, then back at her, "I just can't live without you. If anything ever happened to you, I'd be lost."

She reached out and brushed his hair back from his forehead and smiled.

"Well, don't worry. I'm not going anywhere. Like I told you all those years ago—you're stuck with me for life."

He smiled and wrapped his arm around her. She leaned against him with a sigh, feeling that at that moment all was right with the world.

"You're right," he said, after a peaceful moment of silence. "Our second honeymoon is much better than the first."

She laughed. "Just think how wonderful our third honeymoon will be."

"Absolutely. Shall we come back here in twenty years?"

"It's a deal."

And they sat in silence, arms wrapped around each other, watching the sun set against the ocean as the last day of their honeymoon week came to an end.

Chapter Nine

Summer 1975

Even the most magical vacations or second honeymoons eventually must come to an end. However, they hardly had a moment to look back wistfully on their Tahiti trip. There was no shortage of writing and research to immerse themselves in once they got back to America, reunited with their children, and settled back into life in their Virginia home. By the time the Jefferson-Hamilton book was published in early 1975, they had eased into a comfortable rhythm of partnership in both their marriage and their professional lives that seemed as if it would last forever.

And then, suddenly, she received an offer that changed everything.

She walked into the living room one evening, carrying two drinks, one of which she handed to Jack. He was intently reading his notes for the new book he was planning and only briefly looked up as he accepted the glass and turned back to his pages. Maybe now wasn't the best time to bring this up, she thought; he seemed distracted, and perhaps wouldn't be able to give the conversation the attention it would require. But she had been waiting to talk to him for days, and there had never seemed to be a good opportunity. Caroline had graduated from high school just a few weeks earlier, and the celebration of this milestone for their older daughter had preoccupied them both. Now she had embarked on her next adventure; John was out with friends on this Saturday night; and Aurora was at a sleepover. It seemed this was the best or in any case the least hectic moment they were likely to find to talk, just the two of them.

"Jack, can you put that down for a moment? I need to talk to you."

He looked up, pulling off his reading glasses and nodding. The lines around his eyes had deepened, and she noticed for the first time that the gray hairs that had begun to appear on his head a few years ago now outnumbered the brown. When had that happened? *We're getting older,* she reflected, feeling a bittersweet mixture of nostalgia and gratitude for this undeniable fact.

"Sure. What's on your mind?"

She sat down, wine glass in hand, and twirled the stem around as she considered how best to broach the subject.

"I've been wanting to tell you for a few days; I had a conversation recently that you should know about."

"What kind of conversation?"

"An unexpected one." She smiled slightly, keeping her eyes on the glass as she sloshed the wine around, being careful not to let it spill. She decided she might as well be direct; there was no point dancing around the subject any further.

"Tommy Guinzberg at Viking Press reached out to me a few weeks ago, and he asked me—" She took a deep breath, then finally raised her eyes to meet his—"He offered me a job as an editor at his publishing house."

She looked directly into her husband's eyes, waiting for his reaction.

He shook his head. "Well, that is big news."

"Yes. What do you think about it?"

"What do you think, Jackie?"

She felt caught off guard, unprepared for this discussion, even though she'd rehearsed it in her head for days. "Well, I mean, it's certainly a flattering offer, but I don't know."

"What don't you know?"

"I don't know if I want to accept. Or even if I should."

His brow furrowed, and he looked puzzled. "Why not? It sounds like a great opportunity for you."

"I suppose, but Jack, I haven't done anything like this in a very long time. The last time I had a regular job was before we got married. That's twenty-two years ago now."

"What does that have to do with anything? It's not like you're not capable. You're a brilliant editor, Jackie. And I know that better than anyone, since you've been mine for the last six years." He smiled.

"For longer than that, really." She smiled back, but then her face grew serious again. "But that's one of the things I need to consider, isn't it? If I were to take this job, we couldn't keep working together."

He nodded. "Which would be hard for me. But for you, I think this could be an extraordinary opportunity."

"Really?"

"Sure. I mean, writing books about American history is fun for me, but it probably gets a little one-note for you after a while, doesn't it? You have so many interests; I know you only stick with these books to humor me. If you went to Viking, you could work on all kinds of different projects. I'd think you'd jump at the opportunity, to be honest."

"Yes, that's true, but—"

"But?"

She sighed and took a sip of her wine at last. "I don't want to feel like I'm abandoning the work we do; like I'm abandoning you."

He shook his head. "Jackie, I appreciate that; I really do. But what about you? What do you want? It's okay to think about yourself first for a change."

She gazed into his eyes, trying to formulate her thoughts. Somehow, she realized, their professional relationship and their marriage had become inextricably intertwined over the past six years. The work they'd done together made her proud from a professional perspective, but more than that it symbolized the new partnership they'd created after they'd left the White House behind. It had been their shared second act. Now, if she struck out on her own, would things change between them? Would their new, deeper connection begin to fade?

And yet she couldn't help being tempted by the Viking offer. It had indeed been a long time since she'd done anything like this; taken on a professional challenge solely by herself with no connection to Jack. She had quit her job at the *Washington Times-Herald* in 1953, shortly before their wedding, because well-bred young women of her era were expected to give up any professional aspirations in order to attend to the business of becoming wives and eventually mothers. But there'd been a part of her, even back then, that had wondered about the trade she was being asked to make. Was there any way she could have held onto her work, her own identity as a journalist and photographer, as she stepped into her new life as a young bride and a member of the Kennedy family? She'd known at the time that the answer was no, but that didn't mean the possibility hadn't danced in her brain a bit, tempting her with a different kind of future than the one she'd been brought up to believe she was destined for.

And now perhaps, after all these years, that life was possible for her after all. Maybe she could seize this opportunity to discover how it would feel to stand on her own again, not as a senator's wife or First Lady of the United States or her husband's collaborator in turning out historical biographies. Maybe it was time, finally, for her to do work that was exciting and meaningful to her, for no one except herself.

"I don't know. I mean, yes, this could be a great opportunity. I think I'd really like to try it."

"Well then, I think you should."

She sighed, shaking her head. "But what about you? And us? Is this going to change things? I mean, everything will be different if I do this. We won't be working together all the time like we have been. I guess there's a part of me that doesn't want to give that up."

Her husband nodded, looking thoughtful. "You're right, things will be different. It won't ever be the same, writing without you. But that's my problem, and I'll figure it out. Meanwhile you have a chance to do something that could bring you much greater professional satisfaction, and I think you should take it. Seize the opportunity. They don't come along that often in life, and I wouldn't want you to look back some day and regret that you didn't take it because you felt obligated to me."

"I am obligated to you. You're my husband, Jack."

"But that's a different kind of obligation." He smiled, and she saw a new understanding in his eyes that years ago she would never have imagined him capable of.

"Jackie, it's been amazing working with you these last few years. Because you're my wife, yes, but also because you're incredibly smart and talented, and the world should get a chance to see that. So, I'm officially releasing you from your professional obligation to me." He smiled, looking a bit sad but also resolute. "You deserve this, Jackie. You've stood by me and supported me for more than twenty years in every way you possibly could. Now it's your turn."

She laughed softly. "So you're officially firing me as your editor?"

"No. I'm sending you off to pursue bigger and better things, and I know they're ahead for you. But don't get the wrong idea. You may not be my editor anymore, but you're still my wife. I'm not releasing you from that obligation. Not a chance."

She set down her glass, stood up and walked towards him, and wrapped her arms around him, leaning her head against his shoulder. "Till death do us part, right?"

"Exactly." He smiled, and turned toward her, and that was the last thing either of them said for a long time.

———————

The next few weeks were a whirlwind. She quickly realized this wasn't just a matter of accepting a new job and return-ing to the working world after more than two decades' absence. On its own, that would have been intimidating enough. There were also logistics to arrange and plans to be made. First, they needed to find a house in New York City, since the commute from their home in Virginia would be impossible. They had briefly discussed whether they should sell the house, but in the end she couldn't bring herself to part with it.

"It's been our home for the past six years, ever since we left the White House," she remarked to Jack wistfully. "And we've been so happy here. Let's keep it, at least for now; maybe it can be our weekend retreat when we need a break from the city?"

He smiled. "Sounds good to me."

She was glad he felt the same way she did about the house, since moving there had never been his idea. As their last months in the White House had ticked down, Jack had let her take charge of figuring out where they would land to begin their next adventure. Looking back now, she could see that his accommodating behavior had been less about being a supportive spouse and more about the fact that he had likely been completely flummoxed about what to do and where to go once his presidency was over. But he'd raised no objections to the Middleburg house, and she knew that even if it wouldn't have been his first choice of place to live, he'd eventually come to like it well enough.

Now, they were moving again—to New York, to another place he hadn't chosen and probably wouldn't have picked if her new job hadn't made it inevitable. She felt some pangs of guilt about uprooting their family to pursue this new opportunity, but Jack insisted that everything would work out, and she decided to trust that he was right rather than worry about what would happen if he wasn't.

Just a few weeks later, they packed their bags, enrolled John and Aurora in a school in New York City, and moved into their new apartment on Fifth Avenue. The next chapter of their lives was about to begin.

———

Friday night finally arrived, and with it the end of her first work week since 1953. She had thought she would feel exhilarated, even triumphant, upon reaching this small milestone, but when she returned home that evening she felt more exhausted than anything else. It was hard work, she had quickly discovered, to be invisible, even as everyone covertly watched your every move.

At dinner that night, she sat quietly as their cook served the meal and let her husband and children do most of the talking. Jack was full of questions for John and Aurora about school, and he managed to get them to open up about their first week, which had included a few normal bumps but had mostly gone smoothly. They both seemed to like their teachers and classes, and they'd begun making friends, reassuring her that this transition wouldn't be as difficult for the two of them as she had feared. By the time the children had finished recounting their school stories, dinner was over, and they'd gone into the living room to watch TV.

Once they were alone for the first time that evening, Jack turned to her. "And what about you?"

She smiled, fidgeting slightly with her napkin. "What about me?"

"How about your first week? Tell me how everything went."

"I told you already."

"No, actually, you didn't. You've hardly said a word about it all week. What's going on?"

"Nothing." She looked down at her half-finished dinner.

"It was easier getting answers out of our teenager." He shook his head, looking seriously at her. "Really Jackie, how is the new job? What do you think of it so far?"

She paused, reflecting on how to describe these past few days.

"Well, there's a lot to learn, a lot of new things to pick up. I can tell I'm going to be very busy. But Tommy has been helpful; he's shown me around, introduced me to people . . ." Her voice drifted off, a bit uncertainly.

"And what about your colleagues? What are they like?"

She smiled, rather sadly, "I don't know."

"You don't? After a week? No conversations at the water cooler to report back? Come on, I haven't worked in an office in years; you've got to give me something." He grinned at her.

She smiled, shaking her head. "That's just the thing. They won't—"

She sighed, and he reached out and brushed a strand of hair back from her face. "What, Jackie?"

She turned and looked at him, then said, "They won't talk to me."

He looked puzzled. "What do you mean?"

"I mean that, exactly. They—my coworkers, I mean—don't talk to me or look at me. No, that's not true. They do look at me, then they look away like they're embarrassed to be caught looking. And then they walk in the other direction, as fast as they can. I might as well be invisible."

He frowned. "I'm sorry, but I'm sure it'll get better soon."

"Will it?" She looked at him, biting her lower lip. "I mean, it's only been a week, but honestly, I'm not sure how much more of this I can take, Jack. It's so bizarre. I mean, I understand that maybe people might feel resentful of me, just turning up at this job out of the blue with no real qualifications or credentials . . . "

"Stop right there," he objected, shaking his head. "You've been editing books for the past six years—even longer, counting all the work you did on *Profiles in Courage* when we were first married. You know what you're doing, and you're excellent at it. Don't doubt yourself, Jackie. You have no reason to."

"I appreciate your support, Jack. But you're my husband. You're supposed to say that."

"Yes, but that doesn't mean it's not true."

"Okay, maybe you're right. But still, this is new to me. This type of work, being in an office again for the first time in decades, and I worry that people think I'm just there on a whim, or that I'm just in my role as decoration. Former First Lady decides to try her hand at editing, just for fun, but who knows how long she'll stay? Will she get bored? And is she even good enough to be here in the first place, over so many other women who could have this job?" She sighed deeply. "I just feel—I don't know. I want to be successful at this, Jack. I want to make the most of this opportunity. And I'm more than willing to work hard and pay my dues, but how can I do that if people won't even speak to me? It's going to be impossible, if this is how the job is going to be every day. One week in, and I'm already exhausted."

He thought for a moment, then looked up at her. "You know, I think you may be reading this situation the wrong way."

"How do you mean?"

"You're assuming that people aren't talking to you, that they're avoiding you because they doubt your abilities or they're resentful of your being there. But I think it's much more likely that they're just intimidated by you."

"By *me*?" She looked genuinely surprised. "Why on earth would they be?"

He shook his head. After all these years, it seemed, she still couldn't see it.

"Because you're extraordinary, Jackie."

She looked startled for a moment, then laughed. "In what way, exactly?"

"In every way." She shook her head and began to speak, but he continued. "Really, Jackie, think about it. You're the former First Lady of the United States, and you're the most famous woman in the world. You've charmed world leaders and heads of state, including plenty I couldn't make any progress with at all, if you remember. You refurnished the White House, you brought the Mona Lisa to America, and somewhere in there I think you may have won an Emmy award, though it's kind of hard to keep it all straight. People are fascinated by you, drawn to you; they always have been. There's just something about you . . ." He broke off as if trying to find the right word. "You're special. You're remarkable, and yes, you are extraordinary."

She smiled at him, her delight in his words lifting her mood a bit. "Well, I don't know if all of that is true, but thank you for boosting my spirits. I just wish that people would stop focusing on all of that and just treat me like a regular person. That's all I want right now."

"I know." He nodded in understanding. "And I'm sure it will happen if you keep doing what you're doing: showing up every day, working hard, letting everyone see how good you are at your job. The novelty of working alongside the most famous woman in the world will wear off for them eventually. And then they'll get to see the best side of you, the woman who wanted to take this job and seize the opportunity to do something she loves, and they'll realize how lucky they are to have you there. And until then, well, just play the long game and wait it out. And if it gets to be too much, we can always go back to Middleburg for a while so you can ride your horses."

She laughed and wrapped her arms around him. "Thank you, Jack. And, yes, I think you're right. Anyway, I've come this far, and I'm not going to give up. People will just have to get used to the former First Lady showing up in the break room for coffee and chasing down manuscripts from them, because I'm not going anywhere."

"That's my girl." He smiled at her and pulled her into his arms.

Chapter Ten

Columbia Presbyterian Hospital, New York City
July 1982

The nurse walked into the room where the family were gathered. As she pushed open the door, they all looked up at her expectantly, awaiting news.

"President Kennedy has just gone into surgery," she told them, her eyes focusing on the former First Lady in what would always remain one of the most surreal memories of her long career. "We expect the procedure will take about two hours, and then he'll be brought into the post-op area and back to his room to rest. You're all welcome to wait here in the meantime, of course."

Mrs. Kennedy nodded calmly, her face a mask that revealed no emotions. "Thank you very much. We will stay here until it's over. And as soon as it's possible, I want to see my husband."

"Of course." The nurse nodded. "We'll share an update on the President's condition as soon as the doctors have finished the operation."

She nodded again, her large eyes fixed on the nurse intensely for a moment before the woman discreetly left the room, and she turned towards her children.

"Don't worry," she said, smiling serenely as she looked at the three of them in turn. "Your father is going to be fine. I'm certain of it."

She caught the look that passed between her children in response to her words with its clear message: *Mom's in denial.*

She knew what they were thinking, and she understood why they were afraid. Seeing their father wheeled into an operating room to undergo surgery would be frightening at any age, and they were still so young, really: Caroline was twenty-four, John, twenty-one, and Aurora, just seventeen. The thought of possibly losing him so early in their lives was no doubt unthinkable to them all.

But that was the point; it was unthinkable precisely because it hadn't happened, and it wouldn't. Not today. Of that she was absolutely sure.

Caroline wrapped her arm around her mother, John took her hand, and Aurora leaned against her other shoulder, the four of them forming a single entity for a brief moment as they began their vigil, waiting for news.

She was so glad to have all her children here with her, and she knew that despite their own fears they were all trying their best to support her. If only there were some way to convey to them that she wasn't crazy or ignorant of reality. It was just that she'd been here before. And she knew things that the three of them didn't know. Caroline and John had been such small children on that awful day nearly twenty years ago now when Jack had been shot. They had, thankfully, no real memories of it. And of course, Aurora hadn't even been born yet. It felt like a bygone era now, a snapshot in a long life—nearly thirty years of marriage, filled with highs and lows, many small, quiet moments that blended into one another as the days and years passed.

But there were still some moments she would remember forever, and the promise that Jack had made to her on that fateful day was one of them. And that was why today she remained an island of calm in the midst of the sea of anxiety that swirled around her.

Everything would be all right. She knew that, because he had told her so, nearly two decades ago.

It had begun about a month ago, or at least that was when the situation had reached its breaking point. Over the past twenty years his back troubles, dating back to his youthful football injuries and the aftereffects of his PT-109 boat sinking during the Second World War, had slowly gotten worse. Every year it was a bit harder for him to straighten up, more difficult to walk without pain; the days when his ailment didn't make its presence known in every movement were becoming more and more elusive.

But in the past year or so he'd noticed that things were rapidly getting worse. The long, slow decline seemed to be hastening, and his efforts to ignore the messages his body was sending him had become all but impossible.

Jackie, of course, could see all of this. Every time she noticed him wince when he sat down in his rocking chair or tried to rise from bed, she would tell him, gently but firmly as only she could, "Jack—you know you can't go on like this forever."

But go on he had, because he saw no other choice. He'd long since given up hope that there was anything his doctors could do for him. The surgery that had saved his life back in 1954 hadn't gotten rid of the pain, and his advancing age was making it worse every day. But what was the point of complaining? At least he was alive, and still able to move, however stiffly and painfully. This must simply be the price of getting old, a price that in his youth he'd never really believed he'd live long enough to have to pay. And yet, here he was.

After months of worsening pain he'd done his utmost to ignore, the final straw had come on the day of Aurora's high school graduation, when he'd awoken to realize that no matter how he shifted and contorted himself, he couldn't get out of bed.

"Jack," Jackie exclaimed when she walked into the bedroom and witnessed his struggle to sit up and put his feet on the floor, "you have to see the doctor. You can't put it off any longer."

He grimaced. He knew she was right, yet it didn't change the fact that he couldn't lift himself up without excruciating pain. He realized there was no way he could possibly see his daughter walk across the stage to accept her diploma. And that made him feel far worse than the searing pain in his back possibly could.

"I'll stay here with you," Jackie promised as she helped him ease his way back down onto the bed. But he shook his head, which only made his pain more acute.

"No, no, you have to go. We can't both miss her graduation ceremony." He saw the conflicting emotions cross her face, but she knew that he was right. One of them had to show up to proudly support their daughter today, and clearly it wasn't going to be him. But he could still read the hesitancy in her eyes.

"Are you sure you'll be okay?"

"Yes. I'll be fine. It's not so bad now that I'm lying down, really," he lied, hoping she wouldn't call him out on the veracity of this assurance.

She looked at him skeptically, but there was no other choice. "I'll be back in two hours. Don't move an inch until we're home, all right? Please?"

"I promise." He managed a half-smile, more of a grimace, but it was the best he could do for now.

"Promise you'll take lots of photos. And bring the camcorder with you."

"Of course I will. And Bobby and Teddy are coming too, and so are John and Caroline. We'll make sure you don't miss a thing."

He sighed. "Tell her how sorry I am. I'll make it up to her, I promise."

"I know you will." She turned from where she stood in the doorway to their bedroom and looked back at him with a resolute expression he hadn't seen in her eyes in years. "And Jack, when I get back, we're going to talk about this. And we'll figure out a way to fix it."

He smiled wistfully. If only it were as simple as she made it sound. But he knew from long years of experience that now was not the time to argue with her. "Okay. I'll be here when you get back," he said, trying to make her smile. She raised her eyebrows at his attempt at humor, gave him partial credit under the circumstances, and swept out the door to be the sole parent celebrating their daughter's achievements at a moment they had long expected to share.

After she closed the door, he sighed and admitted that she was right. He couldn't go on like this. It was time to take action.

He'd been looking forward to seeing his youngest daughter graduate from high school for weeks now, especially since she'd brought home the news last month that she would be class valedictorian and as such, tasked with giving the school graduation speech. He hadn't thought he could possibly be prouder of Aurora, who had been accepted to Harvard and would be beginning her studies at his alma mater in the fall. But watching her spend hours toiling over her speech preparations while also studying for her finals had reminded him yet again how remarkable a young woman she really was.

Their last child, on the verge of leaving home. Soon, for the first time since Caroline was born nearly twenty-five years ago, it would be just him and Jackie in the house, with all their kids having flown the nest to make their mark on the world.

If he was looking forward to hearing Aurora's commencement speech, he knew that was nothing compared to how excited she was for him to watch her give it. For weeks now she'd been asking his advice on writing and delivering her remarks. "You *have* done this a few times before, right, Dad?" she'd teased him when he protested that her speech should be her own creation, without his fingerprints on it. "I mean, you can't blame me for trying to take advantage of all your experience, right?"

She'd worked so hard to get to this point and poured so much of herself into writing and practicing her speech. He knew that she was doing so in part because she wanted to make him proud. And now, he was going to miss it. Because of his physical weakness, he wouldn't be there to witness the most important moment of his daughter's life.

And he hated himself and his traitorous, deteriorating body for that.

———

"Well, I have good news for you, President Kennedy," his doctor told him and Jackie as they sat in his office two days after their daughter's graduation ceremony. "There have been some promising advancements in recent years in treating the type of chronic back pain you're experiencing. There's a particular surgery that might go a long way towards alleviating the symptoms."

He was startled, but it was Jackie who spoke first. "Surgery?"

The doctor nodded. "Yes. There are new procedures now that can greatly improve quality of life for patients with long-term back issues. However," he said, sitting down in the chair behind his desk, "I must caution you; there is some level of risk involved."

"What does 'some level' mean, Doctor?"

"Well, the surgery itself is fairly straightforward. We've had high rates of success with many patients who've undergone it over the past few years, and in general the procedure is well-tolerated. However," the doctor paused, looking directly into his eyes, "I should caution you that most of the patients I'm speaking of are younger men and women. Risks of complications rise as a patient gets older, particularly for men; we're not quite sure why that is. And for someone with your medical history, the risks are more serious than they would be for a typical patient."

The doctor ran through the potential risks: neuropathy, potential balance issues, and last but definitely not least, the risk of partial or even full paralysis.

As he spoke the last word, Jackie gasped slightly, and her eyes darted quickly to her husband. He stared straight ahead for a moment, then said, "I think we should discuss this and then get back to you, Doctor Folsom."

"Of course," the doctor nodded. "Take as much time as you need. In the meantime, I'll refill your pain medication, and we can schedule a follow-up consultation in a few days."

As soon as they arrived home and sat down in the living room, he turned to her. "Well? What do you think, Jackie?"

She looked down for a moment, then glanced up again. "This has to be your decision, Jack."

"Yes, but you're going to give me your opinion anyway, so let's just do it now. What do you think?'

She was silent for a moment, as though weighing her words. At last, she spoke. "I don't want to lose you, Jack. No matter how many times I've faced that possibility, it's never gotten any easier—and it never will."

He nodded, waiting for her to continue.

"But I also don't want you to spend the rest of your life miserable and in pain when you don't have to be. The risks of the surgery do sound scary—but I think in this case, doing nothing would be even worse."

He nodded. "That's exactly what I think. And it's true, what you've been telling me these past few months; I can't go on like this much longer."

She nodded. "So, then, we're agreed?"

He nodded. They were indeed, although there was more to his own decision than he'd chosen to share with her. But what mattered was that they were on the same page.

"Yes. I'll call Dr. Folsom and schedule the surgery as soon as possible."

———————

Two weeks later, he was lying on a stretcher in a hospital gown, silently remembering all the times he'd been in similar situations before and devoutly hoping that however today's procedure turned out, this was the last time in his life he'd have this particular experience.

I'm getting too old for this.

His children, grown into young adults before his eyes seemingly overnight, sat with him and their mother during the pre-op period. Jackie was keeping the rest of the family—his brothers, sisters, nieces, nephews, and his indomitable, seemingly indestructible ninety-one-year-old mother—updated on the news, but he'd refused their offers to come visit him today. There would be plenty of time for that afterward, he'd assured them all, making light of his upcoming surgery as much as possible. He could only hope that his confident prediction would prove true.

As the medical staff came to whisk him off to the operating room, Caroline, John, and Aurora hugged him one more time and quietly filed out of the room. Jackie, however, remained seated by her husband's side, as if refusing to leave until she was explicitly told to do so.

He turned to the nurse approaching his bedside. "I'd like a few minutes with my wife, please."

"Of course, Mr. President." The nurse nodded with professional courtesy and a touch of human understanding, and she and her colleagues left the room, shutting the door behind them.

He looked at her for a moment in silence as the sun, in a hopeful omen, burst brightly into the room through the half-open curtains. The golden light seemed to dance around her face, making her look ethereal.

He took her hand, smiling at her. "You know, I swear you're aging backwards."

She looked surprised, then laughed, shaking her head. "I promise you that's not true."

"Well, I'm sure I've given you a few gray hairs these past few weeks, but overall . . . ." He shook his head. He knew she thought he was just flattering her, as a good husband of thirty years should, but it was more true than not. Three decades after they'd first met, she still possessed a radiance, a magic even, that he'd never encountered in any other women he'd ever known.

He hadn't been totally upfront with her about why—despite the minimal but still real risks—he'd been so determined to try this surgery. Of course, it was partly to alleviate his worsening pain and to ensure he'd be able to live the fullest life possible in the years that remained to him, not trapped by his own body's weakness in a barely tolerable existence. But there was more to it than that. Looking at his wife now, he felt the twelve-year age gap between them more deeply than he ever had before. In the past, when they'd been in their twenties and thirties and forties, it had felt like nothing at all, and he couldn't have imagined how the seemingly slight gap would appear to widen bit by bit as they grew older. As a young man, envisioning the future had never been his strong suit.

But now he was sixty-five years old, officially a senior citizen. "Don't worry about it, darling," Jackie had teased him a few months ago when he'd mentioned his upcoming milestone birthday and how old the encroaching number made him feel. "You'll qualify for all the senior discounts now—just think how much money that will save us!" But her jokes aside, and however much she assured him that he was aging magnificently (as wives of thirty years were supposed to do), the fact remained that he was, if not yet elderly, certainly on the off-ramp to it, while she was still in the prime of her life.

And the past few years had been spectacular ones for her. After returning to the working world seven years ago, following her long hiatus during which she had, as he liked to say, made a profession of making him look good in every way possible simply by standing next to him, she'd enjoyed success after success, redefining herself for a new stage of her life. Jackie's career as an editor, first at Viking Press and now in her current position at Doubleday, had given her the opportunity to bring countless new books to life and indulge her intellectual curiosity as never before. She loved her work, and she loved New York City and their Fifth Avenue apartment in almost equal measure. At just shy of fifty-three, it seemed as if Jackie were hitting new heights every year, and as much as he missed working with her on his own books, he knew she'd made the right decision to strike out on her own. He was proud of her, and thrilled that the entire world could now see her as the powerhouse he'd always known her to be.

And yet it was precisely his pride in her and his awareness of how hard-won her personal and professional happiness were that made him determined not to stand in her way in the years ahead. He refused to let himself wither into a feeble old man when she still had a full life ahead of her.

As he gazed at her now, the light framing her face made her look like a young woman, scarcely older than she had been during their White House years. Those long-ago days had been filled with many highs but also plenty of lows, many of the latter of his own creation. But now things were different. She was happy; they were happy. He wanted their life together to continue just as it had these past few years for as long as possible.

And yet, the realities remained. He was sixty-five; she was barely fifty. She might live another forty years, long enough to see their children reach the age he was now, to welcome their great-grandchildren into the world. By that time, he would no doubt be a memory. But in whatever time he had left, he would not hold her back. He refused to let her take on the role of caretaker to her aging husband when there was so much else in the world left for her to experience.

He hadn't told her any of this when he'd made his decision about the surgery, and he didn't say any of it now. If he raised his concerns about their future, he knew she'd shake her head and respond as she always had: *till death do us part.* And he knew she meant it, just as he'd meant the promise he'd made to her in the backseat of the limo in Dallas nearly twenty years ago. And he had every intention of continuing to keep that promise for as long as he could. But when the time came, whether today or in the distant future, when he could no longer do so, he wanted to die knowing that he'd never been a burden to her, never kept her from living her life to its fullest and being all that she could be.

He broke into his own reflections. "Remember what I said to you that day?"

She nodded solemnly. "Yes, I do. And I'm holding you to it. This isn't your time, Jack—not even close. We have years left ahead of us. I'm sure of it."

He smiled, nodding. "So am I." And that was the truth.

Just then the doctors and nurses returned and wheeled him off to surgery. She held onto his hand as long as she could until it slipped out of hers as once again he headed for the operating room. As he felt the anesthesia begin to kick in, the surgeon asked him to count backwards from ten. But in those last seconds of awareness before the drugs pulled him under, instead of mulling over numbers, he recalled the words he'd spoken to her that day two decades ago and the promise he'd spent a lifetime since then keeping.

I won't leave you, Jackie.

———————

She sat silently, counting the minutes on the clock on the wall of the hospital waiting room as they ticked by. She tried not to think about what was happening at the moment, only what would happen soon. Her husband would be returned to her, safe and whole, with a better, happier future ahead for them both.

He would. He had promised her, and she was certain that once again he would keep that promise, at least if it was in his power.

But no. Today was not the day she would lose him. Just as it hadn't been the day thirty years ago, or twenty years ago. Jack had faced more challenges over the course of his life than any man should ever have to, and yet he continued to persevere. He wouldn't be going quietly today either; of that she was absolutely certain.

He's going to come back to me. To all of us.

After what seemed both an interminable age and no time at all, the surgeon appeared in the doorway and made a discreet sound to get her attention. All four of them looked up, anxious and expectant.

"Well, Mrs. Kennedy, I'm happy to report that the surgery was a success. The president is in the post-op recovery area now and is doing well."

She didn't realize she'd been holding her breath until she let it out, feeling the relief flood her as the tension that, in spite of everything she'd been telling herself these past few hours and weeks, had been building inside her until this moment was finally released. She turned to her children, feeling tears welling in her eyes even as she smiled at the three of them, and then looked back at the surgeon.

"Thank you," she responded, her voice barely more than a whisper. She forced her normal tones out, feeling as if she'd almost lost the use of her voice. "Thank you so much. May I see him?"

"Yes, you can go in for a few minutes. He'll be resting for the next hour or so, then we'll bring him back to his room. Depending on how the post-surgery recovery process goes, we hope he'll be able to go home in a few days."

"Thank you so much." The doctor nodded, smiled, and left the room. She turned to her children, beaming at all three of them.

"You see? I told you everything was going to be fine, didn't I?"

They all nodded, smiling joyfully and hugging their mother one by one.

"So, can we see Dad soon?" Aurora asked, wiping a stray tear from her eye as she looked at her mother expectantly.

She nodded. "I'm going to see him for a few minutes, and then we'll all be there when they bring him back to his room, okay?"

They nodded, and she followed the nurse out of the room towards the recovery area.

And there he was. Lying on his back, hooked up to an array of tubes and wires, but looking alert and still managing a smile for her after everything he'd just been through.

"Hello there," she said, smiling broadly as she sat down next to him and took his hand in hers. "I hear you came through the surgery with flying colors."

He grinned. "That's what they told me."

"How do you feel?"

"Not bad. Mostly numb. No idea how many drugs they've got me on right now. But I can't complain."

"The doctors say the surgery was a complete success. And now you're going to begin to heal, and soon you'll feel better than you can imagine."

He nodded. "Here's hoping. But anyway, I made it through today."

She smiled, running her hand through his hair, which was now completely gray, with the occasional bright silver strand poking through. The sight reassured her—the visible proof that her husband was still here, aging as he was supposed to, outlasting so many predictions and near-misses and catastrophes. He was, without question, the strongest and most resilient man she'd ever known.

"Yes, you did. And there will be many more days to come, once we get you out of here. There's lots of life left in you, Jack."

"You're right. I'm not going anywhere anytime soon, kid."

She smiled at his nickname for her from the earliest days of their marriage. "No, you're not. I have your promise, and you're not allowed to rescind it. There's too much ahead for us and our family. We need you here for all of it."

He nodded and closed his eyes for a moment; she could tell the medications must be starting to make him drowsy. "It's okay, go ahead and sleep. I'll sit here and stay with you until they kick me out, and then they'll bring you back to your room soon to rest. The children will be so happy to see you; they've been so worried, even though I told them everything would be fine."

He nodded slightly, and she could see him beginning to drift off to sleep.

"I'll stay with you," she repeated softly, stroking his hair. And she would, she told herself. Until the very end, whenever that day might be.

Till death do us part.

Chapter Eleven

Hyannis Port, Massachusetts
May 29, 1992

T he return of summer felt real and tangible at last. The sun shone brightly, the salty Cape Cod air rode in on a light breeze, and a festive mood prevailed among the large group of family and friends who had turned out today for the party to kick off the summer season and celebrate a milestone birthday.

This particular celebration might have seemed normal, even mundane, except that from the moment he'd woken up this morning and opened the presents excitedly presented to him by his granddaughters, he'd been reminded that this was no ordinary birthday. The number on the card that had accompanied his gifts was an unmistakable reminder of that fact: *seventy-five*.

Today, he was seventy-five years old. Running the number through his head, trying to make sense of it, wrap his mind around the passage of so much time, felt beyond him. He'd woken up this morning wondering if he'd feel different after crossing this threshold, if any profound insight about the nature of life or wisdom accrued from age would suddenly strike him. But all he could muster was the first thought that had entered his mind when he looked over at his bedside table and saw the handmade birthday card from Rose and Tatiana sitting in its place of honor, the numbers carefully printed in the center.

Seventy-five. That's a lot of years.

More years than he'd expected, certainly. More years than, once upon a time as a young man, he could have imagined even knowing what to do with. And yet, every morning he woke up to the reality that he was, against all odds, still here.

He hadn't planned on a big party, but Jackie, as well as Caroline, John, and Aurora, had insisted that they couldn't let this milestone birthday go unacknowledged. So today, the whole Kennedy clan would gather in Hyannis Port to celebrate with sailing and clambakes and games of touch football he was far too old to join in now, but at least could watch. And while he would have been quite content to leave it at that, another guest would be joining them today, one he had to admit to himself he was curious to meet after all the excitement surrounding his rapid rise to national celebrity over the past few months.

But first his family would assemble to spend his birthday together, and at the moment they were still missing one member. As he stepped out the front door at the sound of the car pulling in, he smiled as she bounded up the steps to give him a hug.

"Hi Dad," Aurora beamed as she pulled back to look him over. "Happy birthday!"

"Thanks, honey." He grinned back at his youngest daughter. "Do I look any older?"

"Hmm; hard to tell. I need to observe you over the course of today to be sure." She smiled at him, walking through the door and sitting down at a seat at the kitchen table. "Where's Mom?"

"She's on the phone with one of her authors. Some kind of revision drama. But she should be down soon. Caroline and the kids are playing on the beach, and your brother is about to gear up for the football game."

She nodded, then burst out with uncontainable excitement, "And what about him? Is he here yet?"

"Your Uncle Bobby? He's setting up to watch the game with your Aunt Ethel."

She shook her head impatiently, her dark hair swirling around her face. "No, not Uncle Bobby. I know he's here. You know who I mean, Dad."

He sat back and regarded his daughter, smiling. "Two former Presidents of the United States at one party not exciting enough for you?"

"Well, you know. I'm used to you guys." She smiled and waved her hand with airy indifference. "But he's quite something, don't you think?"

"I don't know what I think yet. I haven't met him. But yes, to answer your question, he and his wife will be joining us today, and they should be here in half an hour. Or so he said. He may not be accounting for how much longer it can take to move from place to place once you have Secret Service protection all around you."

"That's exciting. But until then, let's catch up, just the two of us. I haven't seen you in ages!"

"Well, that's not my fault, is it? Mom and I have been sitting around the house in New York just waiting for you to stop by."

She looked abashed and shook her head ruefully. "Sorry, Dad. I meant to come by to see you both ages ago. It's just been such a hectic few weeks."

"And how's the new job treating you?"

"Busy, but good so far. I guess I'm still in the honeymoon period, though."

She began excitedly telling him about her first week at her new job as a reporter at *Vogue*—the very same magazine Jackie had long ago turned down an opportunity to work for in Paris after winning a national essay-writing contest during her senior year in college. But had she taken that job, she might never have met her future husband; and as she had said while reminiscing over the story upon hearing their daughter's news, her life hadn't turned out so badly as a result.

He was happy that Aurora seemed to be enjoying *Vogue*, though it certainly marked a departure from her previous professional endeavors. After graduating from Harvard in 1986, she'd paused just long enough to serve as maid of honor at Caroline's wedding that summer before taking off for two years in the Peace Corps in Sierra Leone.

She'd told him she'd felt drawn to serve in the organization he'd started during his presidency to try to do some good in the world and see how things were really done on the ground, far away from the lofty heights of government and academia in America. He'd been proud of her decision to begin her adult life by embracing the challenge and venturing so far from home and her family, and fascinated by the stories she'd brought back with her after her two years overseas.

After returning to America, she had worked for a few small nonprofit organizations, then decided to pursue a career in journalism, getting her master's degree and securing the job at *Vogue*. Her real goal, she said, was to write about stories that mattered, in America and overseas, that people would actually read. *Vogue* certainly promised her an audience, even if she would have to learn to balance fashion pieces with writing about men and women around the globe who were working to transform the world.

"But *Vogue* seems to be evolving its content," Aurora remarked, pouring herself a soda and sitting back in her chair. "Just last month we—well, they, since I wasn't working there yet—did a really interesting article on you-know-who."

"And who would that be?" He smiled, knowing she'd bring the conversation back to this topic as soon as she could.

"You know. Our guest of honor today. Other than you, Dad, obviously." She grinned at him, clearly hoping for more information, but as he'd told her before, there wasn't much more he could say about that yet.

Just then, Jackie breezed through the kitchen door. "Sorry for the delay, but I'm all done with work now and ready to celebrate. Hi, baby!" Her eyes lit up, and she hugged her younger daughter, pulling back to look her over thoroughly. "You look wonderful. How is *Vogue*?"

"So far, really great. But I'm still new; maybe they're saving all the really hard work for my second week."

Jackie smiled. "Did you know that you gave your very first interview to *Vogue*, back when you were a baby?"

"What? No! How did you not tell me that?"

"Well, it's true. You were about a month old, and we did a photoshoot with your brother and sister to introduce you to the world."

"Oh, God." Aurora shook her head, looking mildly horrified. "I hope they don't still have those photos in the files."

"Well, if they don't, I do. They're upstairs in one box or another. We should take a look at them sometime; they came out beautifully. And of course, you were absolutely adorable."

"Thanks, Mom. Anyway, enough about me—time to celebrate Dad's birthday!"

He laughed, shaking his head. "So she says, but she seems far more interested in our guests today than in her ancient father. Which reminds me, they should be here any minute."

He walked to the window to look outside, and as if on cue, several black cars drove up and entered the long driveway. Jackie walked over and stood next to him, shaking her head as she looked out at the motorcade. "I must say, I don't miss those days at all. At least not that part of it."

"Are you sorry we invited them?" It had been in the back of his mind all day, whether this was bothering her. When the idea to extend the invitation had first been proposed, he'd planned to do it on some day other than his birthday, which he would ideally have kept to family and friends. However, after some back and forth, this was the only date that had worked for the visitors. Jackie had responded with good grace as usual, but he hated to feel as if he were foisting unpleasant reminders of a past lived under glass for eight years onto her on what should be a purely enjoyable day.

"No, no." She smiled at him, shaking her head. "It will be fine. We can chat with them for a few minutes, and then they'll probably have to be on their way, so we'll still have the rest of the day for the family celebration. I was just hoping for a little more peace and quiet, but I'll manage."

"If peace and quiet was what you wanted, you married into the wrong family."

She laughed. "Very true, but it's a little late to do anything about that now, isn't it?"

He took her hand, smiling, and they walked out to the porch to watch as the small parade of black cars came to a halt. "At least nothing's leaked to the press about this yet."

"Mmm. Hopefully it stays that way. At least for a little while."

Just then, two figures emerged from one of the cars: a blonde woman who strode calmly and confidently toward the front door and a man who, though clearly trying to maintain some solemnity, seemed to bounce forward in their direction with all the youth and vigor he remembered possessing himself decades ago. As they reached the front door, flanked by their entourage, this guest reached out his hand, looking—for all his clear confidence and self-assurance, well-deserved after his recent victorious campaign—a trifle awestruck, unless he was just imagining that reaction.

"President Kennedy," he said, speaking in a rather raspy voice with an Arkansan twang that had become familiar to the country over the past few months, "It's truly an honor to meet you. Mrs. Kennedy, you as well. Thank you so much for allowing us to join you today."

He put out his own hand, nodded, and smiled at both of their visitors. "Of course. It's a pleasure to meet you, Governor and Mrs. Clinton."

As the four of them finished shaking hands and expressing their pleasure at meeting one another, he ushered them inside. His head was full of thoughts and impressions and memories, but as they walked past the kitchen table where he and Aurora had been chatting just a few minutes ago, he noticed she was gone now, probably outside with her siblings as the football game kicked off, and thought, *She's going to be so mad at herself for missing this.*

He'd introduce them all later. Right now, it was time for the Kennedys and the Clintons to get to know one another.

———

"I'm sure you don't remember, sir," Governor Clinton said as the four of them sat down at one end of a long table in the dining room, looking out over the Cape Cod shoreline through a broad picture window, "but this isn't the first time we've met."

"Really?"

"I visited the White House when you were President, back in 1963. I was sixteen, and there was a ceremony in the Rose Garden for Boys' Nation participants. You shook my hand and said a few kind words to me; I still have the photo. It's framed in my office at the governor's mansion back in Arkansas."

Jackie glanced at her husband, suppressing a smile. She knew he'd be pleased by this tribute.

"Well, that's quite something," he responded, shaking his head. *How the years fly.*

After a few more minutes of small talk, Jackie stood up. "Mrs. Clinton, I'd be delighted to show you around a bit, if you'd like to join me for a walk on the beach?"

"Of course," Mrs. Clinton replied, standing and smiling at the former First Lady. The two of them quickly exited the room, leaving their husbands alone together.

"Congratulations on a hard-fought campaign, Governor," he said, with a slightly wistful smile. "It was a very impressive victory. Well done all around."

"Thank you, Mr. President." Clinton bobbed his head with a kind of deference he rarely showed to anyone. "It's been quite a ride so far—but of course, there's still lots of hard work ahead."

He paused for a moment, biting his lip and running a hand over his hair. "And that's why I wanted to see you today: to ask for your advice, anything you can share with me that you think would be helpful. You've done this, twice, and to be honest, your presidency is what inspired me to go into politics and public service in the first place."

"That's good to hear. I think you have the opportunity to do great things for the country, Governor."

"I hope so. But first I have to win the general election this November. And that's why I'm here—to ask you for your support. I understand you stayed out of the primary race, but now that I've wrapped up the nomination, I'd be honored to have your official endorsement."

He nodded, smiling. "I don't think my wife will be upset if I reveal that both of us have been watching your campaign for a while, and to be honest, we've been rooting for you to win. And now that you'll be carrying the torch for the Democratic Party in November, I'll be glad to stand behind you all the way. You've got my endorsement, Governor, and I think it's safe to say, Jackie's as well."

"Thank you, President Kennedy. That means more than you could possibly know. And now I have one more favor to ask you."

And with that, he made his second request—the real reason he'd detoured from the campaign trail today to meet his political hero and ask for the kind of help that only the man sitting across from him could give.

Meanwhile, Jackie and Hillary Clinton were walking together along the shoreline, their introductory conversation quickly turning to shared stories about the ups and downs they'd experienced as political spouses and on the campaign trail.

"The worst was when Bill lost the governor's race after his first term," Hillary recalled, shaking her head ruefully.

"We didn't see that coming, and it was hard for us both. But he picked himself up, ran again in two years, and won; and we were back in the Governor's mansion, and it felt like we'd never left."

"Very admirable. The hardest campaign for me was 1964. It had only been a few months since the assassination attempt, and I remember being so afraid for Jack every time he went out into those crowds. And I was pregnant then, so I couldn't be with him on the trail as much as I would have liked. It was very stressful at the time, but as they say, all's well that ends well."

"That must have been very difficult for you," Hillary nodded as she peered intently at the former First Lady. "You know, I want Bill to win the presidency so badly. He wants it more than anything, and so do I. But still, I worry about those possibilities too, about something terrible happening to him."

"Of course you do. That fear comes with the role of political wife, I'm afraid. And I can't say it ever gets any easier—at least, it didn't for me."

Hillary shook her head. "You know, I was only a teenager in 1963, but I still remember hearing the news that day in November and how my family—who were all Republicans, mind you—gathered around our TV after the story of the Dallas shooting broke. And we didn't move an inch until we heard that President Kennedy was going to be all right. I remember what a scary time it was for the country. But for you, I can't even begin to imagine what that must have felt like during those hours before you knew everything would be okay."

"Those were the longest hours of my life." She nodded ruefully, remembering every moment of that horrible day as clearly as ever even thirty years later. But while the memories would never fade completely, she was glad that she'd finally reached a point where the mere recollection of her husband's near-murder didn't make her feel paralyzed with residual terror. That day had cast a long shadow; it had been well over a decade before the nightmares had fully ceased, before she'd finally stopped waking up in a panic in the middle of the night, reaching over to Jack's side of the bed to confirm to herself that he was, indeed, still there.

She shook herself out of these recollections and turned to her guest—and, she felt already, her new friend—with a smile. "But don't be so worried or anxious that you can't enjoy this time. You and your husband have achieved a remarkable victory, against long odds, and you should savor every moment. The campaign trail will be exhausting but exhilarating as well. And I promise it's an experience neither of you will forget for as long as you live."

Hillary nodded thoughtfully. "Mrs. Kennedy, if you don't mind my asking—how did you do it? Not just the campaign, but how did you navigate eight years as First Lady afterward, and do it so well?"

She smiled a bit wistfully, remembering those long-ago days. Being a former First Lady was part of her history, an essential element of her biography, but it was not a part of her life she dwelled on much anymore. Maybe it was because she and Jack had been so young while it was all happening; she was thirty-one, and he was only forty-three when they'd first entered the White House. By the time she turned forty, that era was already part of her past, and they'd both chosen to make a clean break from it as much as they possibly could. Jack's gloom in the wake of leaving office had made clear to them both that the only way forward for them was to focus on the future, not dwell on the past. It was the only way to thrive and find happiness with their family and each other in the years ahead.

But that didn't mean she didn't remember. The recollections, both good and bad, were always there beneath the surface, waiting to be tapped.

"I can't really give you advice," she said now, shaking her head. "Every woman who occupies the role of First Lady is different and brings her own personality and experiences to the job. So all I would tell you is to be yourself as much as you possibly can. Remember who you are apart from your husband's career, even though a big part of the job is to support him in that work. It's a tricky balance, but it's very important not to lose yourself. First Lady is a title; it comes and goes, and no matter what happens you won't have it forever. But you'll always be you, Hillary Rodham Clinton. Make sure that woman remains at the core of every decision you make, every project you take on, everything you do for however long you and your husband may be in the White House."

Hillary nodded thoughtfully. "That's very good advice, Mrs. Kennedy. I do hope I can hold onto my sense of self if Bill and I make it to the White House. And of course I hope I'm able to get my daughter through the experience as successfully as you clearly did with your children."

"Yes, that's very important, and it's not always an easy challenge. It was easier for me, I think, when my children were little; it was simpler to shield them from the press, from the craziness of it all. But as they got older and went to school and made friends, it became more difficult to ensure they had as normal a life as they possibly could, despite where they lived and their father's job. I wanted privacy and normalcy for them so badly; sometimes, trying to provide that felt like a full-time job in and of itself. But I think ultimately we did all right."

"Oh, there's no question of that, from what I've seen of your children. I really hope to emulate the way you raised them and kept them so level-headed in the glare of so much press and publicity, the kind we'll have if Bill wins in November. And I'm sure I'll have many more questions for you if that happens."

"Oh, I think there's a good chance it will." She smiled. "And if it does and you ever want any guidance or advice, please do reach out to me. I'll be happy to help you in any way I can. But ultimately, I have no doubt at all that you'll be a great success as First Lady."

"Thanks for the vote of confidence, Mrs. Kennedy." Hillary Clinton smiled, and as they reached the end of their walk, the two women turned into the house to join their husbands, who were just finishing their own conversation about the past and the future.

"So what do you think of him?"

It was several hours later; the Clintons had long since departed, and his birthday celebration had wound down. He and Jackie were getting ready for bed, this momentous milestone of a day already fading into memory when she finally asked him the question she'd waited until they were alone to pose.

He shook his head; how to begin to answer? Jackie looked at him expectantly, waiting for his response.

"He's smart, that's for sure. Very good at appearing self-effacing when he wants to, but you can tell there's a will of steel beneath the surface. Which he's certainly going to need in the race he has ahead of him." She nodded, waiting for more.

"He's, I guess *charismatic* is the best word to describe someone like that? He's got a presence. But there's substance to him as well. I think he can do a lot of good for the country if he gets the opportunity."

She nodded. "I've always thought that, just from what we've seen of him these past few months. But I'm glad to know you feel the same, now that you've gotten to speak with him. Did you offer him our endorsement?"

He smiled. "Well, I told him he had *my* endorsement, and I imagined, yours as well."

"Good." She smiled, sitting down next to her husband, who was now lying on the bed and staring thoughtfully at the ceiling. She reached out and took his hand. "Is something wrong?"

"No, nothing's wrong. Just thinking."

She fell silent, waiting to see what else he would share. A moment later, he suddenly said, "He asked me to speak at the convention this summer."

"Ah." She said nothing for a moment until her husband's silence prompted her to add, "What did you tell him?"

"I said I'd do it." He turned to her, shaking his head slightly.

"But you don't want to? Why not?" She remembered well the days when speaking before enraptured crowds had been Jack's favorite activity in the world, or certainly one of them, making his current lack of enthusiasm seem a bit strange.

"It's not that. It's just—it's been a while since I've done this kind of thing, hasn't it?"

She smiled. "Twenty years, as I recall." He'd spoken in 1972 at Bobby's first convention but had bowed out in 1976 when it was clear that his brother didn't need any help from him to get reelected handily, as he had been later that year. *I want this to be Bobby's moment,* he'd told her then when he explained his decision, and she had understood.

He hadn't spoken at a convention since, nor had either of them attended one. Their lives today were lived out of the spotlight as much as possible; it was a habit by now, one they'd both settled into. But she knew that part of Jack's withdrawal from the public sphere had been a choice he'd made for her. He'd understood that her worries about his safety, while they'd faded significantly over the past three decades, had never fully gone away, and he'd tempered his own desire to participate on the public stage to allay her fears. He'd put her feelings first, whatever his own might have been.

When she was young, she had believed that love was about grand gestures and dramatic, soul-crushing sacrifices couples made for one another. But now, in her sixties, she felt that perhaps this was what real love—the kind that lasted forty years—was about: finding ways to be yourself while making the compromises you needed to in order to bring peace and happiness to one another. She recalled her comment to Hillary a few hours ago: *It's a tricky balance.* It was indeed, but navigating that balance successfully over the past three decades had brought both of them a deeper, more lasting happiness than she'd ever been able to imagine as a young bride. She was grateful, every single day, that their love story had lasted long enough for them to reach this place. Grateful for the gift of time.

She shook herself out of these recollections. "But so what? So, it's been a while. I imagine it's like riding a bicycle or a horse. You never forget how to do it."

He laughed. "You're the horsewoman in the family. I've never been any good with them."

"But you *are* good at public speaking, Jack. Brilliant, actually. It's one of the things you do best; it always has been. Even if it's been a while since you've gotten any practice in, I'm sure that isn't going to change."

"Well, I hope you're right." He sighed, stretching and looking at his hands, wondering when they had become so gnarled and wrinkled. Another reminder that he was today, for better and worse, seventy-five.

After a moment he added, "You know, I can't remember the last time I saw Aurora as thrilled to meet someone as she was when we introduced her to Bill Clinton today."

"Well, of course. She's excited by him and by what she feels his campaign represents. A lot of young people her age feel the same."

"That's exactly what I mean. Young people today, people Aurora's age, or John's or Caroline's, that's what excites them now. A new generation of leaders stepping up to the plate."

"But that's good, isn't it? It's the way it's supposed to be." She sighed, lying down on the bed and turning to face him. "It's not 1962 anymore, Jack. We can't freeze time and keep things the way they were when we were young."

"I know." He nodded. She was right, of course. But that didn't make it any less bittersweet to see the tide of history rolling forward; the world he'd once helped shape marching on without him, seemingly without a backward glance.

It's the price of getting old. A gift, certainly, but not a pure one. Aging was a privilege, and one that he'd nearly missed out on so many times that he tried never to take it for granted. But despite knowing that, his feelings about this milestone birthday, no matter how fortunate he knew he had been to reach it, were still mixed.

After a moment's silence, Jackie said, "Is that why you're so reluctant to speak at the convention?"

He sighed. "Maybe. I don't know. I guess a part of me wonders if anyone is actually going to care at this point. We left the White House twenty-three years ago. So much has happened since then. The world has changed so much, and—I don't know. To get up in front of a crowd in Madison Square Garden and try to bring back some magic from thirty years ago when half the people who'll be watching were probably kids when I was in office, or not even born yet? I don't know, Jackie. I don't know if anyone will still give a damn, honestly."

"Of course they will. Don't be ridiculous. Why do you think he asked you to do this for him, Jack? He's appealing to young people in the same way you did thirty years ago. He wants you to stand with him and speak at the convention because you've had a powerful influence on his own ideas about what kind of president he wants to be. He wants to inspire a new generation, just like you did. And he's right. It's an honor, and a well-deserved one. I wish you'd see it that way." She reached over and touched his face. "It doesn't make you obsolete, Jack—just the opposite. Your legacy continues to this day, and that's why he wants you there."

He took her hand, smiling slightly. "In other words, it's time for us to pass the torch to a new generation?"

"Yes," she smiled, "I'm sure I've heard that somewhere. Sitting in the freezing cold at your first inauguration, actually."

"You're right. The time has come. So, I guess I'd better get to work on my speech, huh?"

"Absolutely. I'm sure it will be brilliant."

"I appreciate the vote of confidence. But do you mind looking it over when I've finished it and giving me your thoughts? I need your editor's eye on this."

"Of course." She curled up against him, sighing, grateful for the end of another day, the bittersweet passage of another year together. "Happy birthday, Jack."

"Thanks, kid."

"And here's to many more."

"Yes." He had no idea what his final birthday count would be, but he was happy to keep them coming—as long as they could celebrate together.

For the next few weeks he took a break from his latest book project to draft and redraft his convention speech.

It had been a while, and indeed he did feel rusty as he tried to craft the right words. It didn't help that he was on his own now, without a team of brilliant speechwriters to compose his remarks, which he had only to glance over to approve and then to deliver. But that was fine with him. He wanted this to be personal. He wanted to share his thoughts and memories, but also acknowledge the new world he was living in. The end of the Cold War, the collapse of the Soviet Union just last year; an event that during the darkest days of his presidency would have seemed like an impossible fantasy was now an everyday reality. But what did that mean for the future? What kind of world would his children and grandchildren be inheriting and shaping in the decades to come?

He knew it was important to acknowledge the country's current economic state—the recession that was impacting people across the nation and driving a desire for change after twelve years of Republicans in the White House. The opportunity for a new, younger leader to rise up and move the nation in a new direction—yes, it all felt familiar. It was all there, the raw material for his speech, but putting it all together seemed an enormous task, like trying to make sense of the last few decades of his life now that he had the perspective of being able to look back and see how everything had played out, how the old struggles had resolved themselves or continued unabated. The sweep of history, moving relentlessly forward, for time only pulled in one direction.

But maybe, he thought, as he wrote and rewrote the speech late into the night in the week leading up to the convention, maybe that made the lessons of the past, the hard-earned wisdom he could offer the country at this stage of his own surprisingly long life, all the more important. He was, after all, an elder statesman now; there was no denying it. But perhaps he'd been avoiding it to some degree. He'd spent the last twenty years writing books and analyzing the past in detail, but never before had he tried to tie the lessons of history into a speech that celebrated the future and all the excitement and possibility of a world he knew he might never get to see. But that was his task now, and he was determined to get it right. This might be the last time he would ever speak to his country, the nation to which he'd devoted his life. If this was his last hurrah on the national stage, he wanted it to be a worthy one.

Two days before the convention, he handed his final typed remarks to Jackie. She'd looked over the previous drafts and, as always, offered helpful suggestions, but now he waited, feeling a bit anxious to see how she would receive this final version.

After reading through his remarks, she paused for a moment, scribbled something on the first page, and handed it back to him. "It's brilliant, Jack. Absolutely perfect."

"Really? No edits, no suggestions?"

"Not a one. It's perfect as it stands. I can't wait to watch you deliver it."

"Thanks," he said, smiling. "So what did you just write then?" He glanced down at the paper to look at her red-pencil scribble.

"Just a tiny correction. You spelled *antecedents* wrong."

He grinned. "Well, spelling's never been my strong suit, you know."

"I do. Fortunately, you have a few other talents." She smiled at him radiantly.

"So, ready to go to Madison Square Garden for one last convention, Jackie?"

"Yes, I think I have one more in me."

"Me too. Let's do it."

———————

They stood offstage together, listening to the buzz of the crowd as it burst into applause towards the end of tonight's warm-up act, as Jackie had referred to it. *Tonight, you're the main event, my love.* And she'd smiled at him, knowing he was nervous but also that he had absolutely no reason to be, and wouldn't be for long once he stepped onto the stage. *You'll be brilliant. I believe in you.*

They had arrived at the convention last night, watching from their private box the series of speeches by assorted Democratic politicians from far and wide. The children would be joining her there tonight, the first time they'd gotten a chance to hear their father speak in a venue like this since they'd been kids. She'd head up to the box to meet them in a minute, but she wasn't going to leave Jack's side until the very last minute when he was ushered away.

Old habits die hard.

"Mr. President?" said an awestruck-looking staffer, approaching them with a harried look on his face. "They're ready for you, sir."

"Okay. Thank you." He turned to Jackie, managing a smile despite his nerves. "So, see you in half an hour?"

"If you keep it that tight, I'll be very impressed." She smiled. "Yes. See you then. And remember, while you're being brilliant, have fun."

She squeezed her husband's hand and leaned forward to kiss his cheek, then turned and followed the staffer who was escorting her back to the box where her children were waiting.

Five minutes later she was sitting in the front row of the box, with John and Caroline on each side of her and Aurora sitting on her sister's right, when the announcement rang through the building. "And now, tonight's final speaker: the 35th President of the United States, John Fitzgerald Kennedy!"

The room broke into loud, almost deafening cheers. She watched as Jack stepped up to the podium, smiling, waving, acknowledging the raucous crowd for several minutes before the audience settled down, and then he began to speak.

She'd read the speech three times and knew every word by heart. But now, as she listened to Jack deliver his remarks, the unmistakable cadence of his voice sweeping through the stadium, bringing specific emphasis and meaning to every word that it would never have had if anyone else had uttered it, she felt something unexpected, something almost akin to shock.

Because she had forgotten.

She had forgotten he could do this. She had forgotten about the way her husband could captivate a crowd, turning strangers into friends, listeners into true believers. She'd forgotten that he could be so—there was no other word for it—magical.

All these years, she thought she'd known him so well. Better than anyone. And in many ways, she did. But the husband she'd come to know so intimately over the past few decades, as their lives had entwined and their connection deepened when they left the White House behind and settled into their new life far from the spotlight and crowds, was different from the man who stood before her now.

She'd gotten so used to the septuagenarian version of Jack—the writer of historical tomes, the devoted grandfather, the man who'd stood by her side and encouraged her to embrace her own career, who unfailingly glowed with pride at her professional triumphs and successes. She had forgotten this side of him: the man who could captivate an audience just by speaking a few well-chosen words, inspire them to slay dragons and win Cold Wars and create a freer and more peaceful world for all. The man she'd fallen in love with, despite all his flaws, and had vowed to love and stand by until the end.

How could she have forgotten this side of him? That he could do this, captivate a crowd so effortlessly and joyfully? After so many years of quiet exile, he was home again where he belonged, in the middle of the world's beautiful chaos and disarray. A true leader, passing the torch but also leading the call to arms for a new generation. And she realized that there was a part of him, the most important part of all, that was born to do this.

She watched the speech raptly, hanging onto every word she already knew was coming, and felt something she hadn't in more years than she could remember: a fierce, almost overwhelming pride in her husband and all that he could do.

She would never forget this night for the rest of her life. She would never again forget how magical her husband truly was. As she listened to his speech wrap up with its final call to urge the audience and the nation to support the man to whom he was passing his torch, she felt her heart swell with pride.

And then, all too quickly, it was over. She rose to her feet and stood with her children, all of them applauding, and feeling as dazed as the rest of the ecstatic, cheering crowd at what they had just witnessed.

Suddenly, she couldn't wait to see him. He was working his way through the crowd, and it seemed to take forever for him to arrive back at their seats as every single person in the roaring stadium appeared to be clamoring for his attention. But finally, when he reached their box and saw her, he grinned, and she read his silent question on his face: *So, how'd I do?*

There were a million things she wanted to say to him, but at that moment none of them seemed like enough. So she did something that, twenty or thirty years ago, she would never have dreamed of doing. She flung herself into her husband's arms and held onto him so tightly that she felt she might never be able to let go. She realized vaguely that a stadium full of people, not to mention millions of TV viewers and more cameras than she could count, were watching them, but in that moment, she truly didn't care.

She looked up at him, beaming, answering his silent question with her eyes, which she suddenly realized were filling with tears. She touched his face and said, so that only he could hear her, "You were brilliant, Jack. Absolutely brilliant."

And the same man who, thirty years ago, had rarely even held her hand in public, wrapped his arms around her and whispered back words that only she could hear, *I love you.*

And in that moment, for the two of them, everything in the world was right.

Perfect.

Brilliant.

Part Three

The End

1994

Chapter Twelve

January 1994

W hy was it always so cold in these rooms?

He sat still, trying not to shiver, though he knew moving around a bit would warm him up. He shouldn't have taken off his coat; he should have worn a sweater, even if the bulky ones in the back of his closet made him feel like an old man. Which, of course, he was. But he hadn't worn one, though it would have been wise to do so, and now he was freezing.

He should have known better, really. How many times had he sat in a room just like this one, waiting for news, for a diagnosis, for some hint of what his future held. These rooms were always freezing, as if they were trying to simultaneously kill off any germs and keep the human beings inside their walls alive as long as possible, as if you could just freeze death and disease away. If only it were that simple.

Finally, when the cold had reached so deep into his bones that he couldn't help rubbing his arms in a vain attempt to warm himself, the doctor entered the room. He looked like any generic physician, tasked to deliver news he undoubtedly did not want to give. He could read it in the man's eyes, that expression that tried to remain professional even as its opacity made clear that something was wrong.

He knew that look well. He'd seen it more times over the years than he cared to remember. And if he were honest, he wished more than anything that this doctor would turn to him and give him the bad news: after all these years his luck had finally run out, and it was time for him to go.

Instead the doctor looked away from him and turned towards Jackie, who sat still as a statue to his left, awaiting the verdict.

"We have your test results back, Mrs. Kennedy. I'm sorry I don't have better news to give you . . ."

———————

An hour later, they were back home in their Fifth Avenue apartment. He had no recollection of how they had gotten there. His mind felt frozen, far more than his body had in the doctor's office before he'd delivered his diagnosis. The doctor's tone had been slow and steady, his drone almost reassuring. Yet he had caught only a handful of the man's words, and those words did not reassure him at all.

"Non-Hodgkin's lymphoma" had been one of them. "Radiation." "Chemotherapy." "We'll do everything we can to treat this, Mrs. Kennedy." He knew the doctor had spoken every one of those words in his office; they were still rattling around in his brain, and no one else could have put them there. But they still made no sense.

Not her. Not now. No.

He realized, suddenly, that they were both sitting on the living room couch. She hadn't spoken since they'd left the doctor's office—or perhaps she had, and he hadn't heard it because his mind was so full of the buzzing of words he was trying desperately to shake from his brain.

"Well," she said, turning toward him and breaking the silence at last, "That wasn't the news we were hoping for, was it?"

She looked straight at him for the first time, and her expression was somber, but she also seemed unnaturally calm. She was trying to hold herself together, as she had become so adept at doing over the years through any crisis or heartbreak. But he saw the truth in her expression: shock mingled with fear, sadness, and perhaps a trace of resignation. It galvanized him, because he couldn't bear to see that look in her eyes. He had to do something. He had to act.

He reached out and took her hand, twining her fingers with his own. "I know. But you heard what the doctor said, didn't you?" He hoped so, since he certainly hadn't been able to catch most of it through the chilly fog that had swept over him after the doctor's initial devastating diagnosis.

"Yes," she said quietly, looking down at their entwined fingers as if there were a message there that might help today's events make some sense.

"There are treatments. Lots of options, plenty of things they can do. You're young, you're healthy; you're the healthiest person I've ever known. This is going to be okay, Jackie; you're going to be okay. I know you are. We'll get through this together, and everything will be fine. I promise."

His words were not a lie or a false assurance. They were, in his mind, the absolute truth. They had to be; there was no other possibility.

She mustered a tiny smile and nodded. "We'll have to tell the children."

"Of course. We can do that when you're ready."

"All right, but not right now, okay? I just feel like going to sleep now and forgetting about this day. I'm sure things will feel better in the morning. Are you coming with me?"

He glanced at the clock; it was 6:30 p.m. But the sun had set, the January air outside still seemed to chill him from within, and there was nothing else that made sense right now except to follow her into the bedroom and try against all odds to get a bit of sleep before the next day and its harsh realities dawned.

They lay down in bed together, her back to him, and he wrapped his arms around her. He had turned on the heat when they entered the bedroom; he didn't know why it was still so cold. But he held her as close as possible, trying to offer her any bit of warmth he could.

They lay there for hours, both awake but not talking. His mind seemed to have sped up after being released from its earlier fog, but none of his thoughts were pleasant, so he tried to shut them out as he squeezed his eyes closed and wished for the relief of sleep to arrive. As he finally drifted off, he remembered his words to her.

Everything will be fine. I promise.

And it would be, he reassured himself. It had to be. Because there was no other possibility.

The next few weeks seemed to pass in a haze. There were more doctor's appointments, more tests, more conversations with medical experts laying out expectations for what was to come, none of which seemed at all pleasant. But Jackie remained outwardly calm, stoic, and seemingly peaceful—almost too much so.

On the morning of her first chemotherapy appointment, he walked out of the bedroom and was reaching for his coat to put on top of his thickest sweater—let it never be said he was incapable of learning from past mistakes—when he saw her eyes widen in surprise.

"Oh, were you planning to come with me?"

He paused, trying to comprehend the words she'd just spoken, which felt as bizarre and foreign as if she'd started rattling off one of the half-dozen languages in which she was fluent but of which he could only pick out a handful of words. "What? Of course I'm coming. What are you talking about?"

"I just thought . . ." her voice trailed off, as she looked down at the rug beneath her feet, "I mean—you don't need to. I'm sure it won't be much fun for you."

Fun. As if she were talking about a concert or an exhibition she thought would bore him, rather than a treatment she was undertaking to save her life.

"Jackie, I'm coming. Don't be ridiculous."

She gazed steadily back at him but said nothing, and in that pause he felt himself becoming angry, even though he knew that was the wrong reaction. But what was the right response? How could she possibly think he'd be anywhere right now except by her side?

And a tiny voice in the back of his mind spoke the bitter truth. *Because of all the times you weren't.*

He knew this was true. He was all too aware of the many times he'd failed her in the past. But that had been years ago, and they'd been through so much together since then. How could she possibly think that he wouldn't be there for her now when she was facing the greatest challenge of her life? How could she think even for a second that he wouldn't be with her when she needed him the most, as she had been so many times over the years for him?

"All right," she said, glancing down at her watch. "Let's leave now, then, so we aren't late."

She walked out the door a few steps ahead of him, leaving him behind, confused, and more hurt than he could ever remember being in his life.

———————

The following few weeks were an incessant whirlwind of appointments, treatments, and conversations with Jackie's medical team. Looking back on it later, one memory stood out clearly to him from the haze of those tense yet monotonous days.

They were getting ready for bed one evening. It was only 7:30 pm, but she'd spent hours at her chemotherapy appointment today, and he knew she must be exhausted.

She climbed into bed and closed her eyes, leaning against him. He wrapped his arm around her.

"How do you feel, kid?"

She smiled slightly, but kept her eyes closed. "I'm okay, Bunny. Thank you." When they were alone, they'd recently resuscitated their nicknames for one another from their earliest married days; he suspected they were both feeling nostalgic for simpler times.

She opened her eyes and looked at him. "Thank you for everything you've done these past few weeks."

He shrugged. "I haven't done all that much. You're the one with the hard job. I'm sorry." And he was. He wished, fruitlessly, that he could take her place, endure everything the universe had arbitrarily decided to throw at her during what should be the prime years of her life.

She shook her head. "You have. Don't sell yourself short, Jack. You've been here for me every step of the way since all this began, and I can't tell you how much it means to me."

He smiled sadly, gazing down at her. "Surprised you, have I?"

She shook her head again, more vigorously. "No, not at all. I knew you'd support me, that you'd do everything you possibly could to make all of this easier. It's not you, it's . . ."

She broke off abruptly, and he prompted her gently. "What, Jackie?"

She sighed, then said simply, "It's me. I don't know how to do this."

For a second he assumed she was referring to her medical treatments, her current draining task of trying to get better and heal. But then he understood.

"I don't know how to be sick," she admitted, almost as if she were confessing something shameful.

And suddenly it all made sense. For their entire life together, more than forty years now, she'd always been the healthy one. He'd been the one constantly enduring one illness or operation or near-death experience after another. His back surgery in 1954, just a year after they'd been married; his battles with Addison's disease; his near-assassination in Dallas; his final back surgery a decade ago. Through all of it she'd been by his side, assuring him that he'd recover, that this wouldn't be the end. She was good at taking care of him, and he had finally learned how to let her do it without feeling weak or ashamed—able to admit to her and to himself that he needed her.

But the reverse had never happened; she'd never gotten seriously ill. The only times she'd been in the hospital for any extended period were when she'd had the children years ago. And even though their shared grief over Patrick's death and her long process of recovery afterward had been hard, physically she'd always been almost superhumanly healthy. Until now.

"Is that why you didn't want me to come with you to your appointment the first day?" he asked as the pieces came together. "Or did you think I couldn't handle it? That it would be too much?"

She shook her head. "No, not exactly. I wanted you there with me, Jack. And I knew nothing I said would keep you from coming, but . . . " She sighed, looking at him sadly. "I guess part of me wanted to spare you all of that.

Because if anyone knows how hard it is to watch someone you love be sick, it's me."

He wrapped both arms around her and pulled her closer. "Thank you for telling me that. But Jackie, what I said to you all those years ago still applies now, more than ever. I want you to be honest with me about what you're going through and how I can help and be here for you. And I will, you know that by now. Always."

She smiled and snuggled closer against him. "Yes, I know. Thank you, Jack."

Slowly, they drifted off to sleep, exhausted from the day's events. But as he fell asleep, it occurred to him that he hadn't spoken to her the words she was so fond of saying to him: *till death do us part.*

But he hadn't needed to say those words, he reminded himself. Because that wasn't going to happen, not to her, not now, not for years and years. Long after he was gone, in a distant future he couldn't even begin to imagine.

It won't come to that, he assured himself, as he drifted off to sleep at long last. *It won't. It can't. That's not how our story ends.*

For that was the one sacred, inviolable truth he'd come to believe in—the certainty that when the time came for them to part, he would be the one to go first. That was the only way it could be.

Chapter Thirteen

New York City
April 1994

I t had rained all week, but today he woke up to see the sun poking out of the clouds, drenching the sidewalk outside their living-room window with light. It felt like a good, even hopeful, omen. Today was Saturday, and the past week had been a busy one. Jackie had had a chemotherapy session a few days ago, and they'd had another appointment with her oncologist, whose words about her progress had been measured but also seemed to contain some notes of optimism. He had taken heart from that and was trying to enter the weekend in a positive frame of mind.

The weather outside served to bolster his mood, as spring was finally beginning to arrive. In another month it would be his birthday. Perhaps by then all her treatments would be finished, and they could celebrate together in Hyannis Port with the whole family, as they had two years ago on the day they'd met the Clintons. That summer felt like a bygone era now in light of everything that had happened since. But now, for the first time since this nightmare had begun, he felt a bit of hope breaking through like the rays of sunlight outside, and he wanted to hold onto that feeling for as long as he could.

"Good morning," Jackie said, walking out of the bedroom and pulling a scarf over her head. She'd begun losing some of her hair due to the treatments, and while she never complained about that or anything else, he knew she was reluctant for the world to see the reality of what her battle with this disease was costing her. Still, she woke up every morning and met the day with a quiet, stoic air of determination. She continued to work, often bringing home projects and toiling in the evenings to make sure her authors were attended to with the same care and dedication she'd always given them. He knew she was exhausted, but she kept going, almost as if she were afraid of what would happen if she stopped moving. And while he constantly told her she should relax and take it easy, there was still something reassuring in her approach to her illness, in how she continued working as hard as she always had and bringing the same quiet determination to this latest fight that she had to every other endeavor she'd taken on since the day they met. She had always managed to accomplish anything she set her mind to before, he told himself. Surely this time wouldn't be any different.

"Good morning. You look happy today. Sleep well?"

"Yes, pretty well. Did I tell you that Caroline and Aurora are taking me out today?"

He was surprised. "No, you didn't. Where are you going?"

"Just out to lunch, and then we're going to do a little shopping. I think the girls thought I could use a break from—well, you know." She swept her hand as if to encompass all the struggles of the past few months in that gesture.

"I think that sounds great," he replied, and he did. She looked happier than he'd seen her in weeks, and he thought an afternoon with their daughters would be a good way to lift her spirits.

"You don't mind being here alone for a while?"

He smiled, shaking his head. Normally, she would never ask him this question. Ever since the earliest days of their marriage, she had always made a point of carving out time to spend alone, whether reading or painting or horseback riding. It was one way in which they were different; he'd always been far more energized by being around people, whether it was the massive crowds he had spoken to on the campaign trail and on foreign visits decades ago during his presidency, or just his family or friends. Growing up with eight siblings didn't allow for much time to oneself, and from an early age he had gotten used to being surrounded by other people. But Jackie had always been more introverted, cherishing her time by herself. Even as they'd grown closer in the years after leaving the White House, spending far more time in one another's company as both colleagues and husband and wife, she had steadfastly preserved her independent streak, and he'd always admired and respected that about her.

But for the past few months he'd barely left her side. Ever since her diagnosis, he felt compelled to keep her in sight at almost all times, as though she might suddenly vanish if he didn't. But he knew that an outing with Caroline and Aurora would cheer her enormously, and that was what mattered.

"No, I'll be fine. Go have lunch with the girls and enjoy yourself. I can read or try to get a little work done." His latest book, a study on Abraham Lincoln's leadership style during the Civil War, had been consigned to the bottom of his priority list since January, and he'd barely written a word since then. Maybe he could try to make some progress on it today.

"Good luck." She smiled, kissed him, and put on her raincoat and sunglasses as she left the apartment to meet the girls.

As soon as she had departed, he was struck by how empty the house felt without her. He ambled around for a bit, trying to get comfortable and read, but none of the words seemed to stick in his mind, and he knew there was no chance whatsoever he'd be able to write anything. It felt strange looking up and not seeing her sitting opposite him, cross-legged in her favorite overstuffed chair, sweeping her hair back with one hand as she read her book or scribbled notes in the margins of a manuscript. Even for just a few hours, everything felt different in her absence. He sighed, picking up a newspaper and scanning the front page, but knowing that really he was just waiting for her to return home. If his younger self could see him now, he reflected wryly, he'd likely be astounded at the changes that forty years of marriage had wrought in him.

The doorbell rang, shaking him from his reverie. He rose to answer it, and as the door swung open, he saw his son standing before him, smiling slightly, yet looking unusually serious as he gazed into his father's eyes.

"Hi, Dad," John said. "I was just in the neighborhood. Can I talk to you for a few minutes?"

Of course, he realized later, it had all been a conspiracy. His children had colluded amongst themselves to set this all up; Caroline and Aurora taking Jackie out so that John could come speak to him alone without his mother present.

But he couldn't see it at this moment, with his mind focused on so many other things, so he sat and talked with John for a few minutes about the latest news, how his planned new magazine venture was shaping up, and even the spring weather, before his son finally got to the real reason for his visit.

"Dad," John said, leaning forward towards him, his chin resting on his hands, "How are you doing? I mean with everything that's happening with Mom. I know it's been a lot for you."

He shook his head, not sure how to answer the question. "I'm doing all right, I suppose. As well as can be expected. But your mother has just been amazing through all of this."

John nodded silently, looking at his father with an inde-cipherable expression. "Dad, I came here today to talk to you about Mom. There are some things we—me, Caroline, and Aurora—have been thinking about, and we want to make sure that . . . " He paused, then resumed in a quieter voice. "We want to make sure you're prepared for what's ahead."

"I know it's going to be tough while she's finishing her treatments, but I think things will get easier after that—"

"Dad," John said, his voice dropping still lower until it was almost too quiet to hear. "That's what we're talking about. You need to realize that Mom—that she's not getting better."

The words hit him with the force of a hammer, and he shook his head and began talking before John could say any more. "That's not true. You were there at her last appointment—"

"Yes, I was."

"Well, so was I, and I heard what the doctor said. There are still things they can do . . ."

"You heard what you wanted to hear, Dad. What the rest of us heard was the doctor talking about what comes next. There are things they can do, yes, to make her more comfortable and to make this easier, but the end result is going to be the same."

John's voice trailed off as if it were simply too painful to say any more. He shook his head vigorously, refusing to accept his son's words because they simply were not—they could not be—the truth.

He tried to think of some sort of counterargument, but after a moment's silence all he could muster was, "You don't understand, John. You don't know how strong your mother is, how much she's been through in her life." He broke off, suddenly flooded with memories and struggling to keep his voice steady. "If anyone can beat this, she can."

"Dad." John reached out and touched his arm, his voice barely more than a murmur but the force of his words still coming through. "You're right; Mom is strong. She always has been. But that's not what this is about. She's sick. She has a disease, and she's done her very best to fight it, but this isn't a battle she can win. It's not her fault. It's just . . . " He broke off, looking out the window towards the view of Fifth Avenue, then back at his father. "It's just the way it is, no matter how much we wish it were different. Because in the end, no matter how strong and brave they are, everyone dies."

He bowed his head and squeezed his eyes shut, as if not seeing his son speak these devastating words would somehow rescind them, remove them from the air between them where they lingered like poison.

I know, he wanted to tell John. And he did. You didn't reach the age of seventy-six without learning this lesson. He'd been losing people he loved all his life, since he was a young man. His brother Joe. His beloved sister Kick, who he still missed every day. His father. Friends from the war. And two children who had died as babies before he'd ever had the chance to know and love them. At this point, it seemed, there was no loss, no type of death he hadn't experienced. He knew all about that pain.

But this was something else entirely. This was a loss that he couldn't begin to fathom, much less accept. Because Jackie was different. Jackie was the one person he had never contemplated having to live without; the one person in his life whom he simply could not lose.

And yet, John was right.

Everyone dies.

He sat silently for a moment, those devastating yet indisputable words running through his head like a dirge. Finally, he looked up at John. "Is this what you came here today to tell me?"

John shook his head, and in that moment for the first time he felt their roles begin to reverse, as if John were the parent and he the child, failing to grasp an essential truth he needed to understand.

"Not just this, Dad. I wanted to let you know that we all know how hard this has been for you. It's been tougher on you than anyone, we realize that. But the thing is, in the end this isn't about any of us, or not mostly about us. It's about Mom, and doing what we need to do to support her. That's why you need to realize what's happening and be ready to face what's ahead. Because you're the person she needs to be able to lean on now. She won't talk to us the way she will to you; she doesn't want to burden us that way. But you're the person she needs to be able to talk to about everything, and right now, she can't. She's trying so hard to protect you from all of this that she can't tell you how she really feels about what she's going through. It's not your fault. I know how much you've done for her, how you've been there for her since the moment this all began. We all see it, Dad. But now—she doesn't need you to tell her everything is going to be okay anymore. She needs you to realize that it's not, and from there . . . to just do whatever she needs you to do for her now."

He shook his head, not because John was wrong, but because he was absolutely right. And he felt, for the first time in three decades, the bleak reality of his own failure.

All these years, ever since Dallas, he'd been trying to be a better husband, the one that Jackie deserved. And for a long time, he believed he had succeeded. He had survived that day against all the odds, and their marriage had survived too, growing into a connection deeper than he had ever felt with anyone else. Life without Jackie was incomprehensible to him now. He had thought that finally they'd put the ghosts of the past to rest, that he'd become the version of himself she needed and deserved. But now he saw that he'd been wrong.

The truth was that after all these years, nothing had really changed. He was still giving Jackie the kind of love that was easiest for him to give, rather than the kind she actually needed. For the past few months he'd been selfishly clinging to her, determined to keep her with him, refusing to see the fact that she was drifting away from him day by day, irretrievably, through no fault of her own. And what she needed from him now wasn't the selfish kind of love he'd been displaying, but another kind—one that would help her let go—even though the idea made him feel as though his very soul was being ripped in two.

He looked up, tears springing to his eyes, and silently nodded. John stood up. and he staggered to his own feet, feeling unsteady. His son reached over and hugged him, and he paused for a second to collect himself.

"Thank you, John."

John nodded. "We're all here for you, Dad, you know that. I know how hard this is going to be, but you won't have to do it alone. You have all of us, the whole family. Don't ever forget that."

A moment later his son left, closing the door behind him softly, leaving him in a house that had never felt so empty.

———————

He was sitting in his favorite rocking chair in the library, looking out the window at the bright afternoon sunshine, when he heard the front door open and shut again. He'd been wanting her to return home since the moment she'd left, but now he felt unsteady, uncertain of what to say to her.

She walked into the room smiling, and she looked so much happier than he'd seen her over the past few months that he dreaded having to bring up his conversation with John. But he knew he had no choice.

"Hello, darling," she said.

"Did you have a nice lunch with the girls?" he asked, hardly aware of what he was saying.

"Oh, yes, it was lovely. And how about you? What did you do while I was gone? Did you get any work done on the new book?"

He shook his head. "No, I didn't. But I did have a chance to do some thinking."

"Oh?" Her expression betrayed nothing but mild curiosity.

"Can you sit down for a minute, Jackie? We need to talk."

As soon as the words were out, he wished he'd chosen better ones. No good had ever come from a conversation that began that way. But she simply nodded, sitting down on the couch across from him. And he suddenly realized that sitting in his chair with her across from him felt wrong, inappropriate for this moment, and he carefully hauled himself up, wincing slightly as his back pain flared up, and sat down next to her.

"John came to see me while you were out." She looked surprised by this news; clearly Caroline and Aurora had done their parts by not betraying any mention of their plan to their mother. "We talked for a while, and he made me realize some things, things that I've been ignoring or trying to ignore. And he was right." He knew he was fumbling, and that his words probably made little if any sense to her, so he decided to cut through all of this and speak to the heart of the matter.

"Jackie, I'm sorry."

"For what?" She looked puzzled.

"Because I haven't handled things very, well these past few months."

She shook her head immediately. "Jack, what are you talking about? Of course you have. You've been absolutely wonderful, from the very beginning."

He shook his head, because as much as he wanted her words to be true, he knew that they weren't. Perhaps she believed them, though. Perhaps, as she often had in their marriage, she was grading him on a curve; giving him more credit than he deserved simply for showing up, for trying, even if he'd been going about things wrong.

But good intentions weren't enough anymore. She deserved better.

"Thanks for saying that—and Jackie, I promise you, I've been trying. I've been doing what I thought you needed me to do while you've been going through all of this—but I realize now that I was wrong."

"Wrong how?" She still looked puzzled.

He reached out and took her hand, remembering suddenly with that gesture the day, almost forty-one years ago now, that he'd placed her engagement ring on her finger, at a time when life had seemed so full of boundless possibility. When everything had been about beginnings, with no thought yet of endings. In his memory it felt like it could have been yesterday.

"I thought I was helping you, Jackie. I thought that you needed me to encourage you to keep going, to fight, not to give up. But that's not true. You've never needed me to make you strong; you already are. You're the strongest person I've ever known. You've faced every single thing life has thrown at you over the years so magnificently, and you've always made it through. But now . . ."

He bowed his head, and she reached out to touch his face, turning him back up to look into her eyes. And as he did, he realized that John had been right. She knew. She had known for a while, for months probably, what was coming. He was the one who'd steadfastly refused to see it.

He forced himself to speak his next words, despite how painful they were. "Now it's time for me to face the truth. That you're . . . that we're . . ."

He couldn't complete the sentence. But her eyes told him that she understood, that she heard the words he couldn't make himself say.

And suddenly, for the first time since that winter day in the chilly doctor's office, she began to cry. Not a few luminous tears sparkling in her eyes, but real, bone-shaking sobs. The sound seemed to fill the room, breaking through the peaceful silence he'd tried so hard to construct for her, the cocoon he had wanted to use to keep her safe, to keep reality at bay. But the cocoon was broken open now, the deceptive calm shattered, and before he knew what was happening, she was in his arms, her face buried in his shoulder, sobs wrenching from her as he held her as tightly as he could. She hadn't cried like this in years; the last time he'd seen it was the Christmas Day after Patrick's death thirty years ago when they'd both fallen apart together, sobbing in each other's arms over the loss of their baby son and the memory of their stillborn daughter.

And suddenly she began to speak. He couldn't make out the words at first, but then she lifted her gaze, her face tearstained and blotchy, and he heard her. "I'm so sorry, Jack."

"Sorry for what?" he asked, astounded.

"For this. For all of this. For what's happened, for what's coming next . . . " She broke off, then looked into his eyes again, tears falling from her own. "Because I'm leaving you. I'm going to be the one to leave first, and that's the one thing I never thought would happen for us. The one thing I promised myself I'd never do."

"It's not your fault, Jackie. It's not anyone's fault. This is just how things have turned out, for some reason." And he thought of all the times it could have ended differently, all his illnesses and injuries and the day he'd nearly been murdered. She was right; the odds had always been in her favor or, more accurately, in his. The chances had always been that he, with his fickle health and the attempted assassination and his twelve-year head start in life, would exit the world first. They'd both always believed that, even if they hadn't said so.

She nodded, her sobs quieting as she began speaking again. "There were so many times in those first few years when I didn't know if we were going to make it—if we even could." He nodded, not needing her to say any more and grateful that she hadn't. He felt a burning shame for all his past mistakes and the pain he knew they'd caused her. But he also knew those emotions were useless; his decades-old guilt couldn't help her now, so he pushed it away, waiting for her to continue. "But no matter how hard things got, I promised myself I'd stand by you, no matter what. That I wouldn't be the one to leave. I loved you, and I'd promised to spend my life with you, for better or worse. And whatever happened, I told myself I'd stick it out until things got better, because I couldn't imagine my world without you in it."

She paused, wiping her eyes with the back of her hand. "And then Dallas happened—and I was so afraid I was going to lose you, just when it felt like we'd finally found each other again. And you pulled through, and I was so grateful—but in those hours at the hospital I kept thinking, what if I lost you? What if I had to say good-bye to you, raise the kids alone, live the rest of my life without you?"

"You would have done it, Jackie." He spoke the words with absolute assurance, one thing he could cling to with certainty at a moment when it felt like he was drowning. "You would have survived, and you would have raised our kids to be amazing people, just like we did together. That was one thing I always knew: that when my time came, our family would be fine, as long as you were here to hold everyone together."

They sat silently for a moment, contemplating the reality that had befallen them. Because despite what they'd both believed for so many years, their story wasn't going to end with him leaving her behind. And perhaps, he mused, the final gift he could give to her was being the one to bear that burden. Because surely, being left alone by the person you loved more than anything in the world was a worse fate than being the one to leave first.

In any case, he realized, he was about to find out.

She looked at him again, her eyes clearer now, the tears gone. "So, what do we do now?"

He wrapped his arms around her and pulled her to his side, and she rested her head on his shoulder. The next words came out as if he were speaking in a play he'd been cast in decades ago, not realizing he knew the lines until now.

"We accept what's coming; we prepare for it as best as we can. And we make the most of every minute, every single second, we have left together for as long as we can."

She turned to him and smiled, and it was a real smile—not as radiant as the ones that had been captured in her most famous photographs over the years, but it was enough.

"You were right all along, Jackie."

She nodded, understanding. "Till death do us part."

And they sat quietly together, not speaking, but grateful that whatever was coming hadn't happened yet, and that all the time between now and the moment that it did was still theirs to spend together.

It wouldn't be long enough. But no matter how the story ends, it never is.

Chapter Fourteen

New York City
May 1994

T he next few weeks were hard. They were the hardest weeks of his life, filled with doctors' appointments and tests and plans for what was coming next, none of which he wanted to think about at all. But he had no choice. The comforting security blanket he'd been clinging to for the past few months had been ripped away, leaving nothing but cold hard truths he did not want to face. But there was no avoiding them now.

He and Jackie spent every waking moment together, from breakfast until they fell asleep in each others' arms every night. "If you need a break from me, it's okay," he told her. "Just tell me, and I'll make myself scarce so you can have some time alone."

She smiled sadly and shook her head. "I appreciate that, but no. That's not what I want now. Just stay with me, okay?"

Stay with me. As if he would be anywhere else in the world right now but by her side.

"Of course I will, Jackie." *Until the very end.*

But as dark and painful as those days were, as they faced the end in the midst of a beautiful, blooming springtime that felt as if it should harbor only new beginnings, there were happy moments as well. More than he would have imagined there could be.

There were visits with old friends and time with family. Bobby and Ethel came over, bringing food and companionship, and the four of them smiled and laughed and reminisced about the times they'd spent together at Hyannis Port in their newlywed days, so many years ago now, but the memories still feeling fresh and recent as they reminisced. That past was long gone now, but it was still accessible as long as they could share those memories together.

There were dinners with Caroline, John, and Aurora, all five of them sitting around the table as they used to do in their old house in Middleburg and before that in the White House when the kids had been small. They talked and laughed, the kids telling stories from their childhood that he'd long forgotten but were still astonishingly sharp in their memories. Caroline and John told Aurora tales from the White House of things that had happened before she was born or when she was too little to remember, and as she often had, his youngest daughter expressed her frustration that she had missed so much of those magical years.

"I wish I remembered more about living in the White House," she said one evening, laughing as Caroline recounted stories of riding around the grounds on her childhood pony, Macaroni. "I wish I had the same memories the rest of you do. I feel like I missed out on so much."

"You loved the White House, though," Jackie told her. "In fact, you loved it so much that you asked me if we could stay after Daddy's presidency was over. You thought maybe Richard and Pat Nixon would let us stay there and keep our rooms if we just asked them nicely."

"Wow—really? I don't remember that at all!" Aurora laughed, and the rest of them joined in. He'd never heard that story before, and he smiled, shaking his head at his daughter's ingenuity and nerve, even as a four-year-old.

That evening they pulled out old photographs that Jackie had carefully preserved, remembering the good times they'd had during their eight years in the White House. And as he looked around at his family, laughing and reminiscing and finding happiness in each other's company despite the dark future that they all knew lay ahead, he felt, for the first time in weeks, something akin to gratitude.

Because he so easily could have missed all of this.

There had been a moment, the morning after his talks with John and Jackie, when he'd woken out of a restless sleep and, for an instant, wished he wasn't there. For the first time since Dallas, for a split second, he'd regretted that the bullets aimed at him that day hadn't killed him as they were meant to do. Because then he wouldn't have to live through any of this.

But looking around at Jackie and their children now, he knew that not only was that a cowardly sentiment, but it was also not a trade he would be willing to make. He and Jackie had had more than forty years together, far longer than he'd ever imagined they would. And while he wished he could go back and do some things differently, overall, they'd had a wonderful life. And he wouldn't have missed a single moment of all the good times, even though it meant he had to feel the pain and grief and emptiness that he knew lay ahead. There was no avoiding that if you were lucky enough to spend your life with someone you loved. One of you was always going to go first. And while he wished, more than anything, that it could have been him, accepting the reality of what was ahead ultimately brought him a strange, oddly comforting sense of peace.

She's still here, he told himself. *She'll be here tomorrow and hopefully the next day, and there are no more guarantees in life beyond that for anyone. So, enjoy these days now, and don't worry about what's ahead.*

He didn't always succeed at this task. But every single morning, he woke up, saw her lying next to him, and knew how lucky he was. And that was enough.

––––––––––

It was a sunny weekend morning in the middle of May when Jackie suggested they go for a walk in Central Park.

"It's a beautiful day, isn't it?" she mused, staring out the window as they finished breakfast. And so it was; bright blue sky, just a few scattered clouds, trees bursting into bloom with their yearly spring flowers, as reliable and predictable as ever. With everything going on these past few months, he'd barely noticed the weather, but it was undeniable today that spring was well and truly here at last.

"Shall we go over to the park? I'd love to walk around for a bit and get some fresh air."

He was surprised but nodded in agreement. "That sounds great. Let's do it."

Ten minutes later, they were walking out the front door of the building, and spring seemed to gently descend upon them like a floral blanket. Trees blossomed with white and pink flowers, showering them as they stepped into the sunlight, and he was incongruously reminded of their wedding. Hadn't someone thrown rice at them that day? Surely that must have happened. What kind of wedding ceremony didn't include throwing rice at the couple? But he wasn't really sure, all these years later, if that had actually happened or was just part of the imaginary past he found himself dwelling on more and more these days. A magical time when they'd been nothing but happy, before the darker realities of life intervened.

Suddenly, out of the corner of his eye, he spotted a slight movement. Before he could turn his head, he felt the flash.

Paparazzi. Just one, it seemed, but one was more than enough.

He supposed he shouldn't be surprised after all these years. Cameras clicking around her had long been something she'd tolerated but never an experience she'd enjoyed. He'd thought, once they left the White House, that this part of life would get easier for her, that the insatiable interest in every aspect of their existence would begin to die down as they retreated to private life. However, the photographers loved her, and clearly the people who bought magazines did too, because there was still a roaring trade in photos of her (and to a lesser extent, him) after all this time. *You're the family star,* he'd joked to her once years ago, after their trip to France and Spain back in 1970 or 1971; his memory for such details was fading. *I'm just your proud escort.*

It had made her smile back then, but it didn't feel a bit funny now. Not when there was so little time left, and his desire to protect her—their—privacy had never been greater. Couldn't they have at least these last few precious moments to themselves? Must everything in their lives, decades after his presidency had ended, be available for public consumption?

But, of course, that was the point, wasn't it? She was ill; everyone knew this by now, if not the details. Any photo taken of her nowadays could be the last one, the last image of her captured for posterity before she moved from real life to history and to memory. They knew this, all the photographers who made their living stalking her for the perfect shot, and that would make them all the more determined to get it while they still could. To capture that very last image.

Vultures. He felt a hot surge of anger rise in him, and he had to fight a momentary desire to confront the camera-wielding pap, grab his instrument out of his hand, and smash it onto the ground. Or maybe, simply smash him in the face.

But when he looked over in the direction of the snap, he realized that the offending photographer was already gone, and he felt his anger dissolve and the reflexive desire to fight, to protect her, drain out of him. Because, ultimately, what did it really matter at this point? Thanks to him, her entire adult life had been lived in the spotlight, and so it would be until the very end. There was no way to change that now.

He hoped against hope that perhaps she hadn't seen it, but she had always had an eagle eye for photographers, honed by years of being hounded by them. A moment later she spoke.

"Well, I guess I've finally found the one sure way to get away from them, haven't I?"

He couldn't think of anything to say to that, so he said nothing, just squeezed her hand tightly.

A few minutes later they reached their favorite spot in the park, tucked away from the crowds and looking out from a copse of trees that provided an outstanding sunset view. She sat down, and he slowly eased himself down beside her, feeling his back ache but determined not to let it distract him, to keep all his focus today on her. But she still saw him wince.

"Are you all right?" she asked, reaching out to touch his arm. Even now, with her own health failing and the last moments of her life approaching with relentless speed, she still worried about him. It felt bittersweet, the knowledge of how much she cared, and the realization that no one else had ever loved him this deeply and profoundly, and no one ever would again. He only wished he'd realized sooner what that meant, how rare and precious that kind of love really was, so that he could have acted accordingly.

He smiled at her. "I'm fine. How are you?"

She looked thoughtful for a moment, as if giving the question real deliberation. "I'm all right. I'm glad we're here. I just felt like taking this walk today for some reason."

"Well, it's a beautiful day." And it was, but he wasn't looking out at the park and its blooming trees or the bright sunlight dappling the green grass. He wasn't even looking around to see if anyone had spotted them here yet. He was staring at her, feeling as if he wanted to memorize her face, every curve and detail of her eyes and nose and mouth while he still could. Because memory was powerful; it could be either a torment or a balm. He had no idea how he would feel once she wasn't here to look at anymore, but he wanted always to keep those memories close and accessible. He never wanted to forget.

They sat side by side, taking in the view before them on this spring day as the sunshine warmed their faces and they looked up at the sky. He was hesitant to speak, to break the peaceful moment, but eventually he turned and looked at her.

"Jackie, there's something I want to tell you. Something important."

She looked at him with a bit of surprise, and then she smiled rather sadly. "Is this some kind of deathbed confession? Because I'm pretty sure I'm supposed to be the one making those."

He shook his head, looking down at the grass. "No, not a confession. Just something I need to tell you."

"All right, then," she said, turning to give him her full attention. "What is it, Jack?"

He paused, weighing what he wanted to say to her and how to say it. For the past few days he'd been going back and forth about sharing this with her; was it the right thing to do? Did it make any sense now? Should he have told her years earlier, and was it now too late to make a difference? The last thing he wanted to do was hurt her, to bring back painful echoes of the past from decades ago. But after turning it over and over during these last few sleepless nights, he'd finally decided this was something he wanted her to know, and he was all too aware that the time to share it was slipping away. It might indeed be now or never. He took the plunge.

"Do you remember—" he paused, then looked up into her eyes, "Do you remember that talk we had the day after Dallas in the hospital?"

She nodded. "Of course I do, Jack. I remember everything about that day."

"And you remember . . . " He paused again, then resumed, "what I promised you?"

She nodded, her gaze steady on his. "Yes, I do."

He nodded. Of course, there had been two promises: one the day of the shooting and one in his hospital room the following day. The first had ultimately proven beyond his ability to keep; but the second had not.

"That day, when I woke up and saw you sitting by my bed, I'll never forget the look on your face, Jackie. You looked shocked and terrified and exhausted, but also so happy that I'd survived. You'd just been through this horrific ordeal, something you never should have had to experience, and yet, all you seemed to care about was that I was going to make it."

"Of course. How could I care about anything else once I knew you were going to be all right?" She reached out and brushed his cheek with her fingers, and he remembered her doing just that in his hospital room that day. Thirty years seemed to fall away in that moment as if they were nothing.

"Well—it made me realize how lucky I was, Jackie. Not only to have survived that day, but to have you with me by my side through everything. And it finally made me understand that things had to change. *I* had to change. I needed to do better, to be a better husband for you, because you deserved it. After everything you'd been through that year— first when we lost Patrick, and then when you watched me nearly die too—after all that, I couldn't stand to do anything to hurt you again. And so I promised you that I wouldn't. And I knew the moment I said those words to you that day that I would keep that promise until the day I died, no matter what."

"And you did." She smiled at him, her eyes full of tenderness, and he reached out and caught her hand as she brushed the hair back from his forehead.

"Yes, I did." She knew that, of course. But there was something more that she didn't know, that he'd never managed to put into words before. Now was possibly his very last chance.

"But the thing is, I thought it would be hard. I thought it would be the hardest thing I'd ever done, that I'd struggle with it every day, that it would be a battle I'd have to find a way to win. And I was prepared for that. Because I told myself that no matter what else happened in our lives, I would never cause you any pain again. I wanted to be the person who protected you from it instead. The way I should have from the beginning."

She said nothing, gazing at him, waiting to hear the rest.

"But here's the thing, Jackie—it wasn't."

"It wasn't what?"

"It wasn't hard." He spoke these words to her at last, what he'd always hesitated to share with her, because he didn't want to bring up the past, to remind her of all the painful early days of their story. "That's what I couldn't believe. Once I told myself that I was going to stop hurting you, to be the husband you deserved after all those years, I suddenly felt—I don't know how to describe it, exactly—but almost a sense of peace. And I realized I'd been wrong all along. Before that day, I thought the only way I could live my life to the fullest was by experiencing everything in the world that I could, no matter what the consequences. But after Dallas, I realized how wrong I was. Because the truth is—you're my world, Jackie. You always were. You were always the only thing I really needed to be happy, the one woman who'd stood by my side through everything, even when I didn't deserve it. I was just too blind, too selfish to see it for much too long.

But eventually . . . " He broke off, feeling overwhelmed by emotion as he spoke these words to her after all this time. "I finally figured it out. And thank God, it wasn't too late."

She sat back for a moment as she took in his words, all the things he'd never said before, because he had been too afraid of digging up the past when it was so much easier to let it lie. And he'd hesitated about doing so until today. Now, looking into her eyes as she processed what he was telling her, he could only hope he'd done the right thing at last.

Finally, she spoke. "Thank you for telling me this, Jack." She looked down at the grass for a moment, running the blades through her fingers, and then looked back up at him and smiled. "And there's something I need to tell you, too."

"What is it?"

She paused for a moment, looking into his eyes. "That day in Dallas, I was terrified I was going to lose you. And once I realized you were going to make it, I was so grateful; I told myself I would never ask for anything else again. And then—" she broke off, shaking her head, "then, you made that promise to me. The one thing I never expected you to say, but you did. And I knew you meant it, with every single fiber of your being. But I also knew that humans are fallible. We make mistakes. None of us is perfect. And I realized that, however good your intentions were in that moment, there was a chance that you wouldn't be able to keep your promise. And I told myself I was all right with that. It was the fact that you would try, that you'd do your best for me, that meant everything. And if you'd fallen short somewhere along the way . . ." She paused, then shrugged. "I still would have loved you just as much, Jack. That's the honest truth. Because I never needed or expected you to be perfect. I just wanted you to be here, by my side, to the very end."

He smiled at her, feeling a bittersweet sense of coming full circle. He'd kept the promise he made to her in the hospital that day, and it had been one of the most important things he'd done in his life. But he realized now that the other promise he'd made to her the day before had been equally important, despite the painful reality that their time together was coming to an end.

Because after all, the length of his life, or hers, was well beyond the control of either of them. And he'd kept his promise all the same in every way that mattered. He had stayed by her side from that day until this one. Not just during the past three decades, which had been mostly joyful and easy, but through the past four months, which had been harder than anything he could ever have imagined as he watched her fight this battle so valiantly. He hadn't been able to save her from what was coming; he was helpless to stop the person he loved more than anyone in the world from dying. He'd once had the power to save the lives of countless people, yet he couldn't save her.

But he realized now that that wasn't the point. Till death do us part, as she'd so often reminded him. That was what mattered—that even as she faced the end, he was by her side, facing it with her. Nothing was more important than that.

I won't leave you, Jackie.

He hadn't. And he never would. He'd do whatever he had to, bear whatever pain lay ahead, to stay by her side until the very end.

He exhaled, feeling himself more weary than he had ever felt before, as if the events of the last few months were finally catching up with him. Well, he was an old man now, no question about that. And if there was one consolation that brought with it, aside from the fact that he'd survived long enough to stay by her side until this final moment, it was knowing that that after she was gone, it wouldn't be long before he followed her on that one last adventure.

She leaned against his side, and he wrapped his arm around her. Somehow, the afternoon light had slipped away while they were talking, and now the sun was setting, the sky catching fire in brilliant orange and purple and gold.

"I love you, Jack," she murmured, closing her eyes for a moment, then opening them up again, because no matter how exhausted she might be today, she couldn't miss this magical sunset.

"I love you too, Jackie. I always have, and I promise you, I always will."

She smiled up at him and nodded before turning back to the spectacular sunset before them that lit up Central Park as it slowly began to sink behind the trees.

If there were any justice in the world, the story would end here—just another husband and wife of forty years watching a sunset together, wishing more than anything to freeze this moment for eternity.

But as the two of them had long ago learned, at great cost, the world was neither just nor fair. And so the moments slipped away mercilessly as they watched the darkening sky, every second ticking down the time they had left to spend together.

But as they had also learned, despite its lack of fairness or justice, this world was still a beautiful place. And so they sat huddled together, arms around one another, watching the sun sink below the horizon and still feeling the same gratitude they'd felt on that November day three decades ago for every single moment they'd been lucky enough to share together, right up until the very end.

Four days later, she was gone.

Part Four

The Aftermath

1994–1998

Chapter Fifteen

New York City
April 15, 1998

He glanced at the clock on the wall of his study: 10:30 am. She was supposed to be here at 11, so he had time to do some work before her arrival, but he wasn't sure that was a good idea. He knew from experience how easy it was to become immersed in his writing, caught up in the act of putting words down on the page and lose track of time. Indeed, over the past few years the ability to lose himself in his work had been a gift, even salvation of a sort.

He glanced down at his notes, squinting to see them without his glasses, the prescription of which had been changed again earlier this year. His eyesight was growing steadily worse, which was hardly surprising now that he was officially an octogenarian. *Put on your glasses,* he could hear her saying in that unmistakable voice of hers. *You know you need them. Don't be so vain, Jack.*

Fine, I will, he replied silently; at least he hadn't yet begun having conversations with himself or with the memories and ghosts that surrounded him every time he set foot in this room. He supposed that it was a victory of sorts, not to have lost his mind and descended into incoherence at this late stage of his life.

You win, Jackie, he thought, smiling slightly as he imagined her slyly grinning in quiet satisfaction as he put on the glasses at last to settle in for a few moments of work. Of course she did. She almost always won these one-sided arguments they would still have occasionally, after all these years.

Being a ghost, after all, was helpful that way.

———————

It had been nearly four years now that she'd been gone. And somehow, unbelievably, he was still here.

The first year after Jackie's death had been a blur. The final months they'd spent together had, at the time, seemed to fly by with impossible haste. But then suddenly everything ground to a halt as the inevitable yet impossible finally became a reality, and the most important person in his life simply disappeared forever.

Looking back, he realized he'd been in shock for much of the first year. It was to be expected, he'd been told by others who'd been through similar experiences. Everything that once made sense to you, everything that once passed as normal life, disappeared, stranding you in a strange new world you couldn't recognize. You'd feel numb for hours or days or weeks on end, and then suddenly the pain would hit you so hard you weren't sure you would survive it.

He had at first responded to Jackie's diagnosis with denial, but then he had determined to be there for her through everything and to appreciate every moment they had left together. That approach had helped him at the time, but it had not prepared him for the future at all. In fairness, he wasn't sure anything could have prepared him for his new existence. Life without Jackie wasn't a concept he could fully grasp while she was by his side, even as he knew their time together was dwindling. It was a binary; a person was alive until they weren't. They were with you, until they left. They were the center of your world until they slipped away to another world altogether, and the world you inhabited without them became unrecognizable in a matter of seconds.

He had spent that first year following Jackie's death mostly trying to survive, fighting not to give into the waves of grief that felt as though they were crushing him, trying to pull him under. It was a terrifying feeling, like gazing into an abyss, but at the same time, there was something strangely seductive about it. How easy it would be to give in to the pull of despair, to simply give up and let himself sink under the waves that felt as though they were threatening to drown him. How easy simply to follow her, wherever she had gone. He didn't know for sure where that was, but he didn't care much either. As long as he could be with her again, location was irrelevant.

And yet, he knew he couldn't give in to the temptation to let himself go. He was still alive, and that meant he was still tied to this world, anchored by the reality of existence. His children needed him. They'd lost their mother, the woman who for so many years had been the center of their family, holding them all together through good times and bad. To allow himself to drift away with her would be selfish. He was still needed here. He knew that. And so he forced himself to stay.

Because after all, surely, it wouldn't be for long.

Finally, the year ended, and another one began. In 1995 his mother passed away at the age of 104, a life that seemed almost biblical in its length as well as in its triumphs and tragedies. As he stood with his children at her funeral and watched her being lowered into the ground, he felt some sense of what John, Caroline, and Aurora had experienced the previous year. How bizarre, he reflected, that his children had lost their mother before he had. It made no sense; it was more proof of the illogic and indifference of the universe. What would be would be, and there was nothing to do but get through it as best as you could.

And yet somehow, that second funeral seemed to snap something awake in him. As he consoled his children over the loss of their grandmother, he felt again the full meaning of being a father. He needed to be there for his children, just as Jackie had reminded him in her final days. *You're going to be their only parent*, she'd murmured to him softly.

They'll need you more than ever. Don't forget that. And he'd known she was right.

Slowly, he felt life begin to return to him in some form, as if the blood in his veins began to move again, if sluggishly. He began bit by bit to remember what it meant to be alive. It wasn't happiness, but the numbness of the first few months began to fade, and he could feel things again, both good and bad. And life slowly began to resume.

In 1996, John got married, and the family gathered to celebrate, trying their best to do justice to the occasion despite the absence of the person they were all silently missing. In 1997 it was Aurora's turn. She'd gotten engaged to her boyfriend of several years the previous Christmas, and after telling her father the news she had asked him, almost shyly, to walk her down the aisle.

"But only if you feel up to it, Daddy," she added quickly, and for a moment he felt his age keenly, seeing himself through her eyes. He'd begun using a cane to get around as he neared eighty, and he moved more slowly and stiffly than he ever had before. But he shook his head at her protestations that she could always ask Uncle Bobby or Uncle Teddy to take on the role of giving her away if it would be too strenuous for him.

"No way," he said, smiling at his daughter. "I walked Caroline down the aisle, and I know I'm a bit older now than I was then, but I can still shuffle down the length of a church. Of course I'm going to do it for you."

She beamed at him, and for the first time in nearly three years he felt a surge of something he'd almost forgotten, an emotion that if not exactly joy was at least an approximation. And in his mind's eye he saw Jackie smiling down at them both, and he realized the image brought him more happiness than pain. Perhaps at last he'd turned some kind of corner.

That April he proudly stood beside his daughter, cane and all, as she spoke her wedding vows and began a new life with her husband, and he remembered doing exactly this in a similar church with Jackie, all those years ago—how long had it been now? Forty-four years. It seemed impossible, and some of the details of that day had begun to fade, but he still remembered. For better or worse, he always would.

———————

He began to write again. It took him a while to resume his work, but gradually he began to turn back to the page, scribbling random thoughts, and eventually he came up with an idea for a new book.

At first, he'd thought the best plan was to find a subject that would allow him to escape, to forget his pain completely. But he soon realized that was impossible. And so rather than find a topic that would distract him from his loss, he went in the other direction. He decided to embrace what he could never forget.

The First Ladies of American History was published in 1997. It was the first book he'd written entirely without Jackie, for even though they'd formally stopped working together once she'd begun her job at Viking back in 1975, she'd never really stopped assisting him by reading over paragraphs, marking up pages, and lending her unerring editorial skills to virtually all the books he'd produced for the next twenty years. "Could you just look over this one paragraph?" he would ask her, and she'd smile, shaking her head, and take the typed pages from him and begin marking them up with her favorite red pen. The writing he produced in his later years hadn't carried her name, but her imprint on it was indelible. She had never stopped helping him create his books.

And he felt her with him as he wrote this one. The subject matter, after all, was inspired by her and all the extraordinary things she'd done during her time as First Lady. However, she did not appear in the story he was writing, at least not explicitly. He knew she'd never want him to write about her, and it was hardly as though he could be objective about her from a historian's perspective, so he chose other notable former First Ladies instead. Abigail Adams, Dolley Madison, Edith Wilson, Eleanor Roosevelt, and a handful of others all made appearances in the book instead. As he retold their stories, he liked to think that their accomplishments were lighting the way for the dazzling young woman who would step into the role in 1961, long after most of them were gone, and make her own indelible mark on the White House and the country. And on him.

Writing, immersing himself in history and words again, helped him to heal. Indeed, those moments when he became deeply involved in his historical research or focused with keen intensity on crafting just the right end to a paragraph or sentence were some of the only times he felt free from his grief. For a moment, or maybe even several moments, he would forget.

And it felt wonderful, blissful even. But of course, it was a trap. Because eventually some fact or tidbit would strike him as so fascinating that he had to share it with her. Then he would turn and look over to his right, expecting to find her there, and it would hit him once again more powerfully than ever that she wasn't. By the time he realized he'd forgotten she was gone, he'd already remembered again, and the moment of surcease from grief was over before it had begun.

She had been many things in her life, but forgettable wasn't one of them. And as hard as remembering could be, he also knew he'd never want to lose his memories of their life together, now that they were all he had left of her.

This is the price you have to pay, he'd tell himself in these moments when forgetfulness ceased, and grief and sadness rushed back in—the price for surviving, for not going first as he'd always believed he would. He was still here, and he supposed he should be grateful. But it didn't stop him from wondering why his life had turned out this way despite the odds. Why this, of all possible outcomes, had been the end of their story.

He began, eventually, to date again, though that was hardly the right term for it. More accurately, he had brief physical relationships with women for whom he knew there was no chance he'd ever develop any kind of deeper feelings. Physical entanglements were one thing; emotional connections were quite another. As he tried to sort through his confusing mix of feelings in the months after Jackie's death, he quickly realized two things: he couldn't live without the physical connection, and he had no interest in pursuing an emotional one. He'd had that already, and he knew that any attempt to recapture what he and Jackie had shared in their forty years together would be futile. But at least for the time being, he wasn't dead yet, and that meant that in some senses life, including that part of it, still had to go on.

He wondered at first how he'd feel about getting involved with anyone else after all these years. Would he feel pangs of guilt at moving on now that she was gone? Would his conscience belatedly haunt him now as it never had done during all his indiscretions in the early years of their marriage?

But it turned out, oddly enough, that the opposite was true. He found that being with other women now, under these strange and unasked-for circumstances for which he was blameless, did not cause him guilt. Instead, in a surprising way, it made Jackie feel closer. He could almost picture her, wherever she was now, shaking her head and smiling as she passed judgment on his romantic choices. *Really, Jack? She's hardly your type. I think you can do better.* In the moments when he could almost hear her voicing these observations from the sidelines, he had to fight the desire to laugh, which would have been extremely inappropriate, to say the least.

Yet there were plenty of nights when he lay in bed alone, trying not to look over at the empty space next to him, and there was nothing funny about those moments at all. It was then, at the end of the day, once he'd finished his writing and read books and watched the news and had dinner with old friends and talked to his children, that he ran out of things to do to make him forget. It made him wonder: what part of his life was real now? Were the routine activities he undertook during the day his real life, and his grief merely a counterpoint? Or was the grief what was real, and the rest of it simply a distraction? It was hard to tell.

As he lay awake at night, he was flooded with memories of good times and bad that they'd shared together. Mostly the memories were good ones, which could bring him either solace or depression, depending on his mood. But what haunted him most, it turned out, wasn't the things that had happened but the ones that hadn't. The times he hadn't been there. The moments he had unknowingly stolen from them both.

When he closed his eyes and tried to sleep on those restless nights, he found himself haunted by the past and his own mistakes. As he thought about Jackie, as the ache at her absence kept him awake and his thoughts drifted back in time, he couldn't help thinking of all the nights in the distant past when they could have been together, but they hadn't been, because he'd been elsewhere—in the arms of other women whose names and faces he could barely remember now, rather than being where he belonged, with the one woman who even in death he could never forget.

He could see now, more clearly than he ever had before, how stupid and greedy and selfish he'd been back then. He'd long ago acknowledged to himself, and belatedly to her, how much his actions had hurt her, and all these years later he was still remorseful. He would forever be grateful that she had been able to look beyond his failures, forgive him for his mistakes, and not give up on him when she had had every reason to walk away. And he was thankful that he had changed course when there was still time to alter the trajectory of their marriage and they'd gone on to have so many happy years together after Dallas. It had taken a narrow escape from a bullet to drive home to him what was really important, and while he knew that a near-death experience shouldn't have been necessary for him to realize that, he was still appreciative that fate, for whatever reason, had seen fit to give him a second chance to be the husband he should have been from the beginning. *It's never too late*, he could hear her saying, though he wasn't sure she had ever actually uttered those specific words to him. It didn't matter; it felt like the kind of thing she would say, and for that he would always be grateful.

But it wasn't only Jackie, he realized now, who he'd hurt with his actions. He'd hurt himself as well. Because moments lost could never be recaptured, even with second chances. Time only moved in one direction, and once you'd lived a day or a week or a month, it was over and done forever, with no chance to recapture those specific moments again despite the best of intentions.

He'd thought he was being so clever, all those years ago. He thought life—or at least that part of it—was a game, and that more was always better. Life was short, and likely to be especially so for him, so why not grab as much of it as he could right now, he had told himself? Why hold himself back from living to the fullest in every way possible?

But that was where he'd made his mistake, he realized now. He'd thought the game he was playing was additive, when in fact it was zero-sum. Every moment he spent with another woman was a moment he could never spend with Jackie once it was over. He'd wasted his time in the wrong places, on the wrong things, for the wrong reasons. And there was nothing he could do to change any of that now.

And so, decades later, he found himself lying in bed alone at almost eighty years old, missing Jackie more powerfully than he could ever have imagined missing anyone, and thinking that if there were a way to go back even for one night, he would do it. He would give anything he had, any amount of money, sell his very soul, for the chance to go back to 1955 or 1956 and spend those fleeting, tragically wasted moments with her. To start again, relive the past, and do it right this time around.

But, of course, he couldn't. What was done was done. Her forgiveness of his actions had been a gift, but it didn't wipe clear the mistakes of the past or bring back those missing days and nights they should have spent together, back when they were young and in love and had everything they needed to be happy. Those nights were long gone, and so was she. And until he could see her again, until they were reunited in whatever the next stop in this strange journey of existence might turn out to be, it felt like lying alone in bed on a cold night, missing her and the past they'd lost and the future that hadn't happened, was some sort of karmic punishment.

He couldn't argue that he didn't deserve it, if that were the case. But that didn't make it hurt any less. And on the lowest nights, he sometimes wished he could simply close his eyes and have it all be over, the loss and sadness and grief lifted from his shoulders forever.

But it seemed he'd have to wait a bit longer for that.

In May 1997, he turned eighty years old. He would have preferred to let the day pass by quietly, but his children and grandchildren were eager to celebrate with him, and he couldn't let them down. So he attended the enormous party they threw in his honor, smiled, and gave a speech poking fun at his own longevity, all the while carrying a secret that he chose not to share with any of them.

The truth was, when he woke up that morning of May 29, he'd felt a strange, unmistakable sense that his time was winding down . . . quickly. This would be the last birthday he would ever celebrate.

He couldn't explain how he knew this to be true. His health was still reasonable for a man his age, especially given the array of medical conditions he had lived with since his youth. Every year he dutifully went into the hospital to receive his annual physical, and every year the doctor ran every test under the sun (or so it seemed to him) trying to detect any possible issues. Yet there seemed to be none other than the general effects of old age. His heart was still pumping reliably, his blood pressure, cholesterol level, and all the other modern indicators of good health were holding steady as well. He couldn't walk as well as he used to, but he could still get around; his eyesight continued to deteriorate, but he could still read and write. And he was eighty, for God's sake. Perfection could hardly be expected from him anymore, and his doctor seemed impressed with his physical well-being when he came in every year. *Everything looks good. Just keep doing what you're doing, Mr. President,* the doctor would say, shaking his head with something approaching admiration.

And yet despite this surprisingly upbeat bill of health, he could tell the end was drawing near. He felt himself moving more slowly and deliberately, his back flaring up and his joints aching more painfully than they had before. He knew these physical symptoms of slow but steady deterioration could only point to one possible outcome.

But it wasn't really his physical state that made him realize the end was drawing near; it was something else, or rather, someone else.

Jackie.

Lately, she felt closer, more present than she had these past few years, as if a wall separating them had begun to thin. She was drawing nearer, he felt, yet he knew that wasn't right. She couldn't come back from wherever she was. And yet the sense of her being closer was perceptible, and one he couldn't shake. He realized that if the gap between them was beginning to narrow, it wasn't because she was coming back to him, which was obviously impossible. No, it was the other way around; he was moving slowly but steadily towards her.

There would be no more birthdays for him after this one, he was certain. And he had no real regrets. Eighty years was a long time to be alive, especially after he'd faced death so often in his youth that the idea of living to be an old man had once seemed impossible.

Ultimately, it wasn't the eight decades he'd now lived that weighed so heavily on him; it was the last four years, the years since he'd lost Jackie. He had survived after her death because he'd had no other choice. But survival as a goal, without her, felt less and less worthwhile as the months and years passed by. It became exhausting after a while, having to push past grief and sadness simply to get up in the morning and keep on living.

Perhaps if he'd been younger, it would have been different: he would have had to find a way to rebuild his life after her, to start over again—maybe even move on with someone else. But at eighty, thoughts of fresh starts felt not only impossible but pointless. He had done pretty much everything during his time on earth that he could have hoped to do: fought in a war, been President of the United States, helped prevent a nuclear apocalypse, raised three children, and spent forty years married to the most extraordinary woman he'd ever known. He'd lived his life, and there was nothing more he could add to it now that made sticking around for another five or ten years of decline feel worthwhile. The fact that it would all be coming to an end soon didn't really sadden him; it brought him a sense of peace.

But there were a few things to tie up before he left. And perhaps the most important of them would finally happen today.

———

He heard the doorbell ring and looked up at his clock: 11:10. It wasn't like her to be late. But then again, she wasn't coming alone; perhaps her companion had slowed her down a bit.

He eased himself up slowly from his rocking chair, hoping to keep his back pain at bay for the next few hours, and walked slowly to the door. When he pulled it open, Aurora stood before him, looking exhausted but also happier than he'd ever seen her. "Hi, Dad! Sorry we're late. This little one took longer than I expected to wake up from her nap and then fell back asleep on the ride over here."

He smiled at her as she pushed the stroller through the door. "You look like an expert already. Very impressive."

"No, I'm definitely still learning. Everything takes so much longer with a baby, but luckily she's a good sleeper most of the time. And I'm slowly learning her ways."

She gestured to the pram where the tiny newborn was still fast asleep. He was anxious to see her but remembered well the rule about never waking up a sleeping baby unless you wanted to incur the wrath of child and parent alike. "Come and sit down, and we can chat till she wakes up."

She sat next to him on the sofa. "How are you, Dad? I'm sorry it's been a while since we've gotten together."

"Well, you've had a few other things going on." He smiled at her, then shook his head. "I'm really sorry I couldn't come to the hospital to visit you." He'd had a slight cold when the baby had arrived six weeks ago, and though he'd been disappointed not to be there, he hadn't wanted to risk passing on any contagions to his daughter and new grandchild.

"Don't be silly, Daddy." She shook her head emphatically, the motion unchanged from when she'd been a boisterous five-year-old. "I'm just glad you're feeling better now."

Just then, there was a slight movement and some noise from the baby carrier—not quite a cry, more curious coos, as if its inhabitant wanted to leave its confines and explore the world outside. "Ah, here we go. She's up." She walked over and picked up the baby, cradling her with expert motions as she moved back to the couch. She pulled the blanket back a bit, so he could see the tiny face properly for the first time.

"Good morning, sleepy girl. This is your grandpa. Dad, this is Jacqueline."

He looked down into the tiny face, the eyes open now and seeming to focus more clearly than a six-week-old should be able to. Of course, he'd known his newest granddaughter's name; Aurora had told him her plans even before her daughter's birth once she found out she was having a girl. And yet seeing her now, hearing that name float in the air between them, hit him more powerfully than he'd expected.

"Do you want to hold her?" she asked, and he nodded silently, his eyes still on the tiny face. It had been a few years since he'd held a newborn, and it took him a moment to get her settled into his arms in the right position, but eventually they both relaxed, and he smiled down at her. He wanted to say something, but no words came; instead, he was flooded by memories.

It felt like just yesterday that he'd held his own children in his arms back when they'd been this tiny. And now he was holding a brand-new grandchild, the first one born since Jackie's death. The first grandchild she'd never get to hold in her own arms and delight in, the first who would never know her, only stories and memories of her passed on by others.

It felt wrong, and as that realization hit him a wave of sadness passed over him, a sense of regret for all that wouldn't be, that could never be again. But as the baby in his arms stared up at him, as though really seeing him, that sadness began to dissipate, and he felt instead a strange sense of calm. There was something in those eyes, wide and bright, that made him feel a connection to Jackie—almost as if some part of her spirit was shining through the eyes of her—their—grandchild. As if she were trying to send a message to him.

I'm still here.

He could hear it, almost as clearly as if she were standing in the room with him, leaning over his shoulder and speaking the words. And he realized that in a profound way, she was. She was here, in this room where he sat with their daughter and granddaughter. She might be physically gone, but her legacy continued. As long as they were alive and remembered her and passed on the memories, she would never truly be forgotten.

And yet he still wished more than anything that she was sitting here with them, holding her namesake granddaughter and smiling down at her alongside him.

He had never felt more conflicted about his own desire, as the days of his life ticked down, to stay or leave. Leaving would mean seeing Jackie again, something he'd wanted desperately since the moment of her death; but staying meant something perhaps equally precious: getting to spend more time with this brand new child, the result of so many distant choices and events from long before her arrival into this world.

Thirty-five years ago, a bullet had nearly ended his life. The next year his daughter had been born. And now she was a mother herself, and this baby with the bright, serious eyes who bore her late grandmother's name was the reminder of everything he'd survived since that nearly fatal day—what could so easily have been the end of his story.

And yet it hadn't been. Here he was still. And he suddenly remembered for the first time in years something Jackie had said to him in the last days they'd spent together. "You mustn't give up, Jack. I know it will be hard for you, and I'm so sorry. But always remember, there are things worth living for."

Now, as baby Jacqueline reached out her tiny fist and he touched her hand as he remembered touching her mother's so many years ago, he recalled those words, and he smiled.

Maybe she was right, he mused. Maybe, at least for a little while longer, there were still a few good reasons for him to stay.

Part Five

The Next Adventure

Epilogue

Four Weeks Later

His bones ached; he was exhausted. He'd stayed up too late tonight, writing away on his latest and most likely final book. He felt a sudden desire to finish it as quickly as he could, for he could feel the days speeding up mercilessly as his birthday approached at the end of the month. He knew time was running short, and he felt more strongly than ever a desire to finish everything he'd started, to keep his promises, to wrap up his eight decades in a neatly finished package before the final moment arrived.

He knew the end was coming, but he didn't know when. He felt mildly panicked about whether he'd have time to finish all the work and say all the goodbyes he'd need to. He'd spoken to all three of his kids on the phone tonight: Caroline had called him, followed by John, and then he'd reached out to Aurora, who had taken a break from the flurry of new motherhood to talk to him for fifteen minutes while baby Jacqueline slept. He'd seen Bobby and Teddy for lunch just last week and his sisters the previous month. He'd tried to squeeze in as many visits with old friends in these past few weeks as he could. He felt he was racing the clock, and he knew that this was irrational—there was no real reason to think that these were his final days, after all. Plenty of people lived past the age of eighty-one. Maybe he would, too. You never knew.

And yet, somehow, he was certain that he did know.

He looked up at the ceiling, squinting against the light in his study, and closed his eyes as if listening for something. He had felt vague echoes through the house all day long, and a persistent feeling that he wasn't alone, though he knew that to be untrue.

He shook his head. There was no point wondering about the future. He'd done his best to tie up all the loose ends of his life, and deep down he felt ready to go whenever the moment came.

And yet.

Something about that sentiment, which he had wholeheartedly believed to be true for so long, no longer felt quite right.

Was he actually ready? Was anyone?

He sighed, put down his pen, took off his glasses, and climbed into bed. What would come would come, whenever it did. In the meantime, he might as well get some sleep.

He still looked the same when he slept.

She gazed down, watching as he closed his eyes, turned from side to side to get comfortable in the bed in their old room where they'd spent so many nights together: the apartment on Fifth Avenue. Before that, the house in Middleburg. The White House. Their various Georgetown houses and Hyannis Port. So many nights she'd lain next to him, watching him fall asleep. Wondering how long she'd have him for, how long he would survive.

Life had certainly played tricks on both of them.

She could smile about it now, of course. For the fears that had possessed her for so long of losing him, of having to live without him, were long gone. And she realized now that in fact she'd never really had to worry at all. Life only had one ending, but ultimately it wasn't a closed door, but an open one. All you had to do was step through.

She knew the moment was coming, and she knew he did too. Of course, his awareness of what came next was far more limited than hers. He didn't know for sure. He just felt, guessed, suspected, tried to tell himself that maybe he was wrong, even though he wasn't. No matter how strong and resilient he was, how many times he'd managed to defy the odds and live another day or year or decade, eventually every clock wound down, and she knew his final moments to be imminent.

It might have made her feel a bit sad, the thought of him leaving this way; all alone, just the opposite of how it had been for her, with all her family and loved ones gathered around to say goodbye. But ultimately, that was just a detail.

Soon, sooner than he could imagine, he'd be in a place where nothing mattered except what was, not what hadn't been.

She knew he'd felt her today; she could see it in his eyes. She knew he could sense her presence. *Only a few more hours, my love*, she wanted to tell him. But even if she could have spoken those words to him, she didn't know if they would be a welcome relief, or a source of pain.

Humans were complicated. Men like him, especially so.

So she waited, as the minutes ticked away on the clock by the bed, and stood ready for the moment to arrive. For him to come to her side one final time.

———————

He opened his eyes and saw the light.

It was a different light than he was expecting—bright yet soft. Not the yellow of springtime sunlight that had been streaming through his bedroom window the past few mornings. It was bright white but not glaring. And somehow it felt too early. It had been nearly midnight when he'd gone to sleep, and it didn't seem as if enough time had passed for it to be morning already.

He looked around and realized his bedroom was gone.

Everything was gone.

He was surrounded by soft white light, but nothing else—no furniture, no objects, no shadows. He felt a few seconds of disorientation, wondering where he could be. But it took him only a moment to put the pieces together.

Of course. Here he was at last.

And the moment that thought occurred to him, before it had even had time to register properly in his brain, he looked up and saw a shape moving towards him, not a ghostly apparition but a real, apparently flesh-and-blood person, the only one he wanted to see right now. The only one, in fact, that he'd really wanted to see for the past few years.

She stood in front of him, held out both her hands, and smiled her most radiant smile.

He gazed at her for a moment, afraid to speak, afraid that if he said anything at all she would vanish as she so often had at this point in his dreams. But she kept smiling, and her eyes never left his, and after a moment he cautiously reached out and took her hands in his. They felt as real as they ever had.

"Jackie," he murmured, wondering if it could be real or if it was just another hopeless fantasy, an illusion sent to tease him until he suddenly woke up and remembered everything. But instead of disappearing, she smiled even more brilliantly, and he heard her voice again for the first time in nearly four years.

"Welcome home, Jack."

"So, are you going to explain all this to me?"

They'd left the bright soft white light behind, and now, somehow, they were sitting in a meadow, filled with lush green grass and flowers. He hadn't noticed how they'd transitioned here, as he'd been too focused on staring at her face, still afraid if he looked away even for a second she would disappear. And despite his feelings of bliss at seeing her again, he couldn't help wondering—was this real? Was this the reunion he'd imagined for so many years, at long last? Or was it a dream, a cruel trick of his mind to lull him into forgetting the bleak reality of life and death for just as long as it took him to wake up and realize he was back where he had been for the past four years, without her?

As these thoughts ran through his still-stunned mind, she smiled at him, taking his hand as she leaned her head on his shoulder. He closed his eyes, squeezed her hand, and decided that either way, at this moment it didn't really matter. If this were a dream, it was convincing enough that he never wanted to wake from it; he'd be happy to live in this alternate world, whatever it might be, forever. Any reckoning with reality could wait. For now, in this moment, they were here together, and that was enough.

"Well," she replied, "as you've probably guessed—this is heaven."

"This place here? Heaven is a meadow?"

She shook her head. "Not exactly. Heaven isn't a place, per se. It's more of—I guess you could say—a plane."

He was thrown by the term for a moment but then understood. "You mean, a plane of existence?"

She nodded. "That's not the ideal word to describe it; it can't really be put into words. But that's close enough, I suppose."

"And you've been here since you left."

She nodded.

"So, what have you been doing all this time?"

She smiled at him. "Oh, this and that. I'll tell you more later. But I've been keeping an eye on you, and Caroline and John and Aurora and the grandkids. But you probably knew that."

He nodded. "I did." He paused for a moment, looking at her more closely. "You look different."

"Really? How?"

He hesitated to say, "You look younger," but it was true. He'd been so caught up in the immensity of seeing her again that it had taken a few moments to register the change. She looked much more like the young woman he'd married nearly a half century ago than the older one whose hand he'd held at her bedside as she slipped away.

She seemed to understand without his needing to explain. "Here, we all look like the best versions of ourselves, whatever that may mean. Young, healthy, unencumbered by aging. It's a gift, getting older, but it does take a toll, doesn't it?"

He nodded, and suddenly realized that for the first time in longer than he could remember, his back didn't hurt, his joints didn't ache, and his vision was perfectly clear again. It was as if they'd both been given a de-aging potion. He certainly had no complaints.

"So, we're young again? Is that why I feel so good, why nothing hurts anymore?"

She shook her head and said in a matter-of-fact tone, "No, that's because you don't have a body anymore."

He stared at her. "Wait—what? Are we . . . are we ghosts?" As he uttered the word, all he could think of was the Casper cartoon his children had loved watching when they were young.

She laughed. "No, not ghosts. Spirits, I suppose. Everything is reduced to its essence on this plane. We don't need bodies anymore, so we can discard them."

"But I can see you. You look just like you used to. How come you still have a body?"

"Well, I don't normally. But it's all about perception. You're still transitioning from the world you left to this one, and so you're seeing me the way you remember me when we were young. But eventually, once you settle in you won't need to do that anymore. And then we'll just be souls, entwined forever."

He pondered that for a moment, then reached out and brushed back a strand of her hair. "But I like seeing you like this. Being able to look at you, touch you. This is what I missed. I don't want it to end, now that we're finally together again."

She nodded in understanding. "I know. But it will start to feel more normal after a while, I promise. Bodies are nice things to have for a while when we're alive. But the problem is they wear out, they start to get sick and cause us pain, and then eventually they stop working altogether. But in this realm, we never have to get sick or grow old or die. We just get to be together with no limits. It's as simple as that."

He smiled at her. "Sounds good to me."

She reached out and touched his face, gazing into his eyes. "Were you very lonely, after I was gone?"

"Yes." He replied without hesitation, then added, "But I had the kids and grandkids and my family, so it could have been worse, I guess."

She nodded in understanding. "And they had you. I was so glad of that. It's selfish, I suppose, but being the one to go first—at least I knew I wasn't leaving them as orphans. They still had their father."

"Yes. But it wasn't the same."

She nodded, then suddenly smiled, her face alight. "Are you ready to see the children?"

He was puzzled for a moment, then understanding hit. "They're here?"

She nodded. "Of course. Patrick and Arabella are both so excited to see you. We knew you'd be here soon. I've told them all about you since I arrived. That's mostly what I've been doing since I got here, spending time with them. I can't wait for you to meet them, Jack. They're both such beautiful souls."

He smiled, and yet felt a trace of sadness as she spoke. "What is it, Jack?"

"It just all feels so unfair." He looked up at her, shaking his head. "I mean, I was alive for nearly eighty-one years. That's unbelievable. I never, ever thought I'd live anywhere close to that long. I was always ready to die young—at least I thought I was. I just assumed that was my fate. And everything that happened in my life, right up until Dallas, seemed to prove it. But then . . . " He paused for a moment, trying to find the right words. "After the shooting, it was like everything changed, and suddenly I couldn't seem to die. No matter what happened around me, no matter who else I lost, I just kept going. And I'm grateful. But Patrick and Arabella didn't get to live any life at all. Not two full days between the two of them. Why not? Why did I live so long, when my children died before they even had a chance at life?"

She nodded. "I know how you feel, Jack. I asked those questions myself when I first arrived here, and if I'm being honest, I asked them many times when I was alive. But after

I'd spent time with them and felt how happy and full of joy and love they both are, it changed my perspective. Life on earth is a beautiful thing, but it's also hard. It's full of love and joy but also sadness and grief and heartbreak. And we both endured plenty of that; every single person who's ever lived has experienced it. But Patrick and Arabella never have. Every single second for them has been full of happiness. They've never known any sadness or pain. Once you've been here for a while and realized what that's like, you can see that it's not the worst thing to spend your entire existence on this plane instead of in the mortal world."

"So, what does that mean? Nothing that happens down on earth while we're alive means anything? Is it all just kind of a waiting room where we live and suffer and learn all the hard lessons until we finally get up here? And if so, what's the point of any of it?"

She shook her head. "No, that's not true at all. What happens down there during our earthly lives does matter. But so much of it is beyond our control. In the end we can only do our best with the time we're given. The world is imperfect, and life can be hard, but all of us can do something, even something very small, to make it better. And leave life at the end knowing that we made a difference."

He was quiet for a moment, mulling all this over. And he decided that, once again, she was right. He'd made plenty of mistakes in life, but as he reflected back now, he'd made good decisions as well. He'd left a legacy that had made the struggles and heartbreaks of his existence worthwhile. And the very best decision he'd ever made, he could see now, was to spend his life on earth with Jackie by his side.

And now, they were together again, forever. He couldn't ask for anything more than that.

He nodded to show that he understood what she was saying, then said, "So, what do we do now?"

She smiled at him. "Well, I think it's time for us to go."

"Go where?"

"Does it matter?"

He smiled. "No, it doesn't." And it was true, but as he spoke the words he found himself pausing for a moment to reflect. He knew it was time to move on, to go wherever the road would lead them. He was ready. And yet.

Down there on earth were so many people he loved, so many people he was leaving behind. A part of him still felt pulled in two directions, between two different planes.

She touched his face again, and he could see in her eyes that she understood. Probably, she'd gone through much the same thing when she'd arrived here. And looking at her now, so peaceful and happy and seeming to almost shimmer before him, he knew that wherever he was going next, wherever she would lead him, would be the right direction.

"Okay, Jackie, I'm ready. Let's go."

She stood up and beamed at him, reached out and took his hand.

And they walked off together back into the soft white light to begin their second life—their next adventure.

The End

Author's Note

The book you are holding in your hands (or reading on your device) is the result of many different threads woven together—a fascination with history; a lifelong admiration for one of my main protagonists; a sort of literary wish-fulfillment; the working through of profound loss and grief; and finally, a boat trip in one of the most beautiful places in the world. (I'll get to that part in a minute).

I was eighteen years old when I picked up my first book on Jacqueline Kennedy Onassis. After becoming acquainted with her extraordinary life story, I went on to devour many more biographies focused on her and her husband. But as fascinating as I found them both, my historical sweet spot for fiction and non-fiction remained the Second World War, and it took me a while to even consider the possibility of writing a book of my own about the Kennedys.

In 2021, I lost my mother after a long battle with cancer. As I tried to process my mom's death, I did something I'd done before at hard moments—I asked myself what Jackie would do. And the answer, of course, was that she would find a way to survive whatever tragedy befell her, to rise above her grief, and to eventually fight her way to some kind of happiness again—the reasons I so greatly admire her.

For the first few months after losing my mom, I coped partly by subsuming my own grief in Jackie's as I devoured any and all materials pertaining to her life—biographies, novels, movies, clips of her giving speeches in Spanish and French on Youtube. I spent a lot of time thinking about grief—mine, and hers—and how unfair it was that she had to carry the burden of so much loss at such a young age, with so many people (an entire country, in fact) looking to her to lead them through the darkness when surely she herself could barely see the way out and through.

Thinking about Jackie during this time did help me—but it also saddened me. And eventually, I began to wonder what her life would have looked like if just one event had turned out differently. What if her first husband had survived his assassination? What if she hadn't had to bury him before the entire world, take on the role of widow and single mother at the age of 34, and spend the rest of her years on earth fighting to move beyond her loss and find joy again? What if she didn't have to struggle through all of that? What if JFK had survived, and the two of them had gotten the chance to, in her words, grow old together and watch their children grow up? What if their story had had a different ending—what would that have looked like?

Of course, we'll never know the answer to any of those questions. But that doesn't mean we can't wonder about them, as I'm sure many of us have. And one day, the seed of an idea that had been growing in my mind for a while took full root—what if I wrote that story, or my fictional version of it?

Around this time, I was lucky enough to take a dream trip to the Maldives. As I floated around on a yacht for a blissful week sailing through the blue seas from one magical island to another, my grief feeling as if it had been left behind me somewhere back in the real world, the story began to blossom in my head in a way I had never experienced with anything I'd written before. Scenes unfurled before my eyes as I gazed at the blue sky on the horizon. Plots began to take shape, characters popped up, and lines of dialogue emerged as clearly as if the real-life versions of my characters were speaking them to me. I knew I had to chase this idea, wherever it might lead me. When I got back home, I immediately sat down and began writing. A year and a half later, I had completed the first draft of my book.

This novel is a story of what might have happened if Jack and Jackie had gotten a second chance on November 22, 1963, and been able to live out the next thirty years together. It is, of course, purely an imaginary version of their story, and an optimistic one at that. I began writing this novel solely for myself, not imagining it would necessarily turn into a full-fledged published book (though I'm very glad that it did!) Therefore, I wrote the happiest future for Jack and Jackie that I felt it was in my power as an author to give them. I couldn't spare them from grief and loss entirely, of course, but I at least wanted to write a story in which we see them face the trials of life together, and where the extra time they receive in this alternate universe gives them the freedom to make choices that strengthen their bond as a couple along the path they walk together.

I had one main rule as I wrote this story: I would only write about things that didn't happen. This book's focus is on Jack and Jackie's marriage post-Dallas shooting, meaning that, of course, every scene involving JFK is purely fictional. While some events in Jackie's story do stay consistent with her actual life (for example, her publishing career and the circumstances around her death in 1994), the focus of these events in the novel is the way she navigates them with her husband. I didn't want to go back and rewrite or attempt to interpret actual history, nor did I want to insert Jack into real-life events he wasn't present for (for example, we can safely imagine that in this version of the story, he walks his daughter down the aisle on her wedding day and attends his children's graduations, but I don't include those scenes as it would have felt weird to me to do so).

This book is also not historical biographical fiction, at least not in the strictest sense. To be clear, I'm a big fan of historical biographical fiction, when it's well done, and especially when it focuses on Jackie! The problem to me is that all these stories about Jackie's life tend to be pretty much the same, since they're working with the same source material (she meets JFK, they date, get married, he cheats on her, she suffers the loss of several children, he wins the White House, she becomes first lady, she lives through his assassination, then remarries, is widowed a second time, starts a new career, and figures out how to move on with her life). It's a compelling story to be sure, but it's been told many times by a plethora of talented authors, and I didn't feel the desire to try to add another similar tale to the pile. This is a different type of novel: an answer to the question of what might have been, if things had only gone slightly differently on a fateful November day.

Of course, there's no way of knowing for sure how Jack and Jackie's story might have unfolded if he'd survived to an old age. I don't claim that my version is the only possible one; there are so many variables, choices, outcomes that we'll never be able to know exactly what would have happened. But this is the story I felt compelled to write, and I like to think it's the future Jack and Jackie should have had—the happier ending they deserved. Not a life free from grief, loss, or pain, because no person's life ever is—but a story that allows them to move forward, together, to a new partnership, love story, and adventure.

I hope you enjoy this story as much as I loved writing it. Thank you for taking this journey with Jack and Jackie and with me.

—*Melissa Kaplan*

Acknowledgments

There are so many people who helped shape, nurture, and develop this book. I am grateful to all of you for the roles you played in helping me take the story I created in my head and turn it into a novel.

First, thank you so much to Bold Story Press, my brilliant and kind publisher, Emily Barrosse, and wonderful editor Nedah Rose. Thank you to Jocelyn Kwiatkowski for all your work on proofreading and production, and to Karen Polaski for creating the beautiful cover. Thanks also to Cathy Bamji, Kelly Schumacher, and the rest of the Bold Story team!

Thank you so much to my first readers, Salimah Perkins and Jennifer Mindek Beckham, for taking the time to read through my early drafts and providing valuable insights and feedback. Thank you as well to Steven Brawley, Alvin Felzenberg, Elizabeth Kern, Monica Klawunn, Edie Myers, Jacquelyn Reeves, and Kris Wortman for reading chapters of the manuscript and sharing your thoughts.

To Alex Baackes—thank you for creating Wander Women Retreats and welcoming me aboard so many times! A week on a boat in the Maldives in 2022 was not only the emotional and physical but also the creative reset I needed to come up with the seed of an idea that, once I was back home, would eventually blossom into this book. It's not an exaggeration to say this novel would not exist without you.

Thank you so much to my lifelong best friend (and brilliantly talented photographer!) Jessica Somers, who not only took my author photo for this book (as well as for my first novel) but was the very first person with whom I shared my idea for this story. I will always be grateful for your support, and especially for taking the time to read through the manuscript and share your insights. I am so very lucky to have a friend like you, and I wish I could transport us back to our hotel balcony in Lake Como with limoncellos in hand right now.

To all of my friends and family (far too many to name)—thank you for all your love, support, and for always cheering me on in my writing. I am so fortunate to have you all in my life.

To everyone who read my debut novel, *The Girl Who Tried to Change History*: thank you so much for taking time to read my first book, and for your eloquent responses to the story. I'm glad to hear that it touched so many of you, and I hope this book will do the same!

Finally, I dedicate this novel to my parents, Rudolph and Josephine Kaplan. You were always my greatest cheerleaders who believed in me no matter what, and your fifty-year love story continues to inspire me (and definitely found its way into parts of this book!) I miss you both so much and wish you could read this story for yourselves, but I believe you are still watching and cheering me on. Love you both forever.

About the Author

Melissa Kaplan was born in Connecticut and has lived for most of her life in the Washington, DC region, where she works in congressional advocacy with a focus on food security issues. She studied at the London School of Economics and Political Science, earning a master's degree in Comparative Politics with a focus on Europe. She has been a passionate student of history her entire life, particularly the World War II era, which helped inspire her to write her first book, *The Girl Who Tried to Change History*. Her second novel, *The Second Life of Jack and Jackie*, was published in spring 2025.

Melissa is an avid traveler who has lived in London and Prague and visited over forty countries. In addition to traveling and writing, Melissa enjoys yoga, barre, and kickboxing classes, as well as reading, working on political campaigns, and planning future travels (and books).

About Bold Story Press

Bold Story Press is a curated, woman-owned hybrid publishing company with a mission of publishing well-written stories by women. If your book is chosen for publication, our team of expert editors and designers will work with you to publish a professionally edited and designed book. Every woman has a story to tell. If you have written yours and want to explore publishing with Bold Story Press, contact us at https://boldstorypress.com.

The Bold Story Press logo, designed by Grace Arsenault, was inspired by the nom de plume, or pen name, a sad necessity at one time for female authors who wanted to publish. The woman's face hidden in the quill is the profile of Virginia Woolf, who, in addition to being an early feminist writer, founded and ran her own publishing company, Hogarth Press.